How the Northern Light Gets In

Six Stories

John Irving Clarke

Grosvenor House Publishing Limited

This book is published by
Grosvenor House Publishing Ltd
Link House
140 The Broadway, Tolworth, Surrey, KT6 7HT.
www.grosvenorhousepublishing.co.uk

This book is a work of fiction. Any resemblance to
people or events, past or present, is purely coincidental.

A CIP record for this book
is available from the British Library

ISBN 978-1-83615-139-5

Dedication

This book is dedicated with love to
Tim and Catriona
whose Northern Light is American

Contents

1. Your Wee Bit Hill and Glen   1

2. Calmness, Courage and Duty   27

3. Touching the Honey Slow River   41

4. The Whole of the Moon   53

5. The Charity of Women   65

6. How the Northern Light Gets In   73

Your Wee Bit Hill and Glen

If you conspire with the devil himself, then all you can do afterwards is run. These were the words that pounded through my head. Run, run, run. And that's what I'd do. I'd leave Black Scaur Farm, take Bess, and with the darkness before dawn masking our flight, together we'd cross the border into England.

I carried the weight of guilt on my shoulders down through the darkness to the basement. I trod cautiously, not expecting anyone else to be about at such an hour and not wishing to cause a disturbance. Bess was there and ready.

"Shush, Bess, shush. This is it. Today."

The previous day I had made sure that she was well watered and fed and I was readying her now for our journey when I heard a shuffling across the straw-covered floor and a figure in the dark made his way towards me.

"Joseph! You had me startled." My voice was little more than a whisper.

"It is today, then?"

"Yes, today."

"In November?"

"I have no choice now. It has to be today."

"You'll be taking Bess?"

For years I had ridden Bess over our farm and to neighbouring farms. When we had worked the bottom field, I had harnessed her to the plough; I had trained her with the halter and bit, I had known her since she was a foal. Why, me and Bess had been bairns together. I had her saddled and ready, yes, I would be taking Bess but she wasn't my horse.

"He's never forgiven you for your mother's death."

No need to establish who *he* was. It was a tale I knew only too well: my mother's death in childbirth and my father's eternal anguish.

"He'll never be able to forgive me now."

Even in that darkened basement stable, I knew that Joseph had registered what I had said.

"Wait then, just a moment."

Joseph slipped out again. How long is a moment? I needed to make a move. I couldn't remain in that place any longer. Joseph would not betray me surely. Bad decisions are made in the face of anxiety and such decisions lined up in front and behind me now.

"Some bread, cheese and pork fat." Joseph was back, bundling packages into my bag. "Don't tell me where you are going, but think south."

"South?"

"South-west. England."

"But Edinburgh..."

He hushed me. "Scotland is keeping troublesome company just now. They will bring about destruction. Sometimes it's best to meet the storm as it is brewing rather than let it overtake you in full force. Go to England."

I had thought of Edinburgh, a little over half a day's ride and then plenty of places in which to disappear.

However, Newcastle would serve just as well, but, not for the first time, Joseph had read my thoughts.

"The English have got an army in Newcastle. The Jacobites are heading that way. There will be trouble. Go south-west. Go to Carlisle."

I looked at Joseph's face trying to read his features in the murky light. My life-long friend and guardian was sending me to England.

"The English are building some fine cities." He handed Bess's reins to me. "Now, I won't open the door for you. You must see yourself out."

"I spoke to no-one. Nobody saw me leave," I told him and he nodded.

"Good luck and God bless." He paid me the respect of not calling me "child."

I closed the great doorway to Black Scaur Farm and rode away without looking back. I knew well enough the fortified farmhouse with the narrow window slits and the huddle of outbuildings. I knew it had been built as a refuge against marauding gangs and raiders and I also knew that its defences couldn't keep out drunkenness and depravity. Black Scaur Farm always had a shadow looming over it. I was leaving and I had a plan.

Over frost-hard ground I was heading for Galashiels. Some stars still winked but over to the east the sky was lightening. Bess's hoofbeats clanged on the earth. I would not be riding her hard. I was content to travel through Galashiels, a lone rider before sunrise, someone would see me but I would pay them no heed. Let them note the figure heading through Galashiels on the drover road to Newcastle. Once through the town though, I would cross the Tweed and double back to pick up the road to Carlisle. At that point I would take more care to conceal myself, pulling my hat low, leaving the road and travelling over open country, through woodland where possible. Speed would not be my greatest ally today.

A market day might have been a different story, but little stirred in Galashiels. The waters of the Tweed were bitingly cold but the river level was low and my plan continued to unfold. To Carlisle, a full day's travel but Bess would get me there.

As daylight broke, the shapes of the landscape began to emerge: the rich pastureland and the rolling hills. Lower down than Black Scaur Farm, there was no reason why farms shouldn't do well here. The market towns and the cities further afield were always ready for wool, grain, milk and cheese. There was no reason why Black Scaur Farm shouldn't have done well except that it was always too easy to sell stock. Fine young foals and calves soon matured into barrels of whisky. It had often been my job to take livestock to a neighbouring farm and if word had ever got back that the agreed price had risen by a farthing or more, I would have been in for a fearful beating. But there was never such a word nor any whisper of me dipping my finger into the cream. Our neighbours embraced trade to everyone's advantage, but with my father it was always business conducted at arm's length with no reason to offer him a tip.

The promise of sunrise had not been kept, the pale disc moon which now dragged me to and fro, was leading to the south-west. Heavy cloud was gathering turning the sky to the colour of an angry bruise. Occasionally, dogs sensing our approach would bark out a warning. Whaups would skitter across fields trilling their ridicule and then stop to point their long, curved beaks. In the high trees, hoodies croaked out the list of charges to be laid against me: embezzler, horse thief and worse, charges, any one of which, could see me at the end of a rope. The accusations swung in the thin air. The long road lay ahead and the sky darkened.

"Am I from my father's seed?" I had once asked Joseph and the delay in his answer I put down to awkwardness, not just the bluntness of my approach. Just when I thought he wasn't going to answer at all, he faced me directly,

"How do you address him?"

"Father."

"Then that is all the answer you need."

We made an effort to resume our tasks, each thinking our own thoughts when he spoke again. "Someday, the farm will be yours."

Joseph was not a man to scorn, but I didn't entertain his suggestion for a slightest moment. If my father had a will, he made no mention of it to me. If he had plans for the farm then they were plans he had not shared. What kind of world would it be if the likes of myself owned a farm such as this?

I continued to ride away from Black Scaur Farm determined to take my thoughts elsewhere. Snow had begun to fall, getting heavier and lying. I wondered whether this would cover my tracks or make them easier to follow. Or whether anyone at all would rouse themselves to seek justice anyway. But the snow was slowing progress and it made the prospect of finding suitable feed more remote. I stopped by a deep running stream where both of us could take water. I ratched in my bag for the bread and cheese and eked out a small portion for myself. Bess turned away from the stream now and began pawing at the settled snow, searching for green grass but it was mostly sedge standing above the increasingly deep snow.

"Come on Bess, we need to change our plan."

I had fondly imagined that we would find a remote sheltered place and see out the night but that had been fanciful thinking for November. What we needed was a proper roof over our heads. How far had we travelled? I wasn't certain. Progress had slowed and I no longer sought to avoid habitations as the snow had driven people indoors. Thin, sharp-edged flakes were being continually caught up in the swirling wind and then flung like stones into our faces. Conditions were worsening, we would not make Carlisle by nightfall.

At first, I thought the but and ben was abandoned but a figure struggling in the field alongside told me otherwise. The struggle was with a horse refusing the pulling and urging, refusing to rise to its feet. In the driving snow, the man kept losing his footing and the horse was resolute. As we approached, our presence had not been acknowledged and I had no wish to startle the man or cause him alarm. Strangers emerging from such foul conditions could not expect a courteous reception. I drew closer to the rundown cottage and saw the byre adjoining. I dismounted, fastened Bess loosely to a low branch and walked towards the man and his horse keeping within their eyelines.

"Can I help?" I had to shout against the wind.

He showed no sign of being startled. He had either been aware of me all along or else he had lowered any defences he had. "We're heading for the byre. Getting out of this."

What kind of horse remains lying down in a sodden field rather than take to shelter in such weather? I knelt down beside her. She showed no sign of getting up and kicking. She was old. Old and weary.

"Have you got any feed for her?" I asked the man and without a word he turned towards the dimly-lit building and I saw in his walk that he too was infirm. In the middle of that field, shielding myself from the harsh flurries of wind and snow, I stroked the horse and watched the man's trudge towards his byre and thought hard on struggle. As Joseph had said to me often enough, *there's no easy life*.

It was feed the horse wanted. I didn't let her have it all at once. I stood and coaxed her up, "This way, this way," and I led her slowly to the meagre shelter and warmth. Her walk too showed that she would be little use now around a farm or even this homestead whatever it was.

"I'd be grateful for some stabling for my own horse for tonight." I had walked his horse into an unkempt stall. There was some space and I had money but I didn't offer any. For the first time, the man looked at me and I saw how the lines of his face carried years of strain.

"I wouldn't turn anyone away on a day such as this. We've room for you and your horse. Maybe you could give us a wee hand before you leave."

I followed him into the main room of the cottage where a thin line of smoke rose from a low burning fire. After the glare of the snow, I was still adjusting my eyes when a voice from a pile of woollen blankets heaped in a chair startled me.

"Robbie! Robbie! Is that you? Where've you been, Robbie?"

"*Wisht*, Father, *wisht*. This isn't Robbie. This gentleman helped me with the horse. His name is..." and he turned towards me.

So much for my plan, I hadn't even thought of a name for myself. "Joseph," I said, "Joseph, but most people call me Joe." The man looked at me as though more was expected but asking would be too forward. "I'm from up Edinburgh way. I have business to attend to in Carlisle."

He looked neither satisfied nor interested. Instead, he nodded towards a pot standing by the fire. "You'll have some crowdie, Joseph?" He poured the thin water and oatmeal mix into two bowls and handed one to me and it was with some alarm that I watched him share the other bowl with the bundled figure. One spoon between them, dipping it into the bowl, feeding him, "There you go, that'll do you good," and then taking a spoonful for himself.

"Who's Robbie?" I asked.

He acted as though he hadn't heard. "That's it. Eat it all up." He continued spooning before he spoke again. "My brother. He saw his fortune elsewhere. He left years ago."

His manner told me to ask no more, and who was I to dig into people's lives? But I only had a fragment of the story.

"Years ago?"

"Aye, many years ago. His body," he indicated to the old man he was feeding, "is sinking into the future but his mind is rooted in the past. He thinks Robbie has just stepped out of the door and he'll be back soon."

Without further invitation, I spent two nights with this man and his father. I bedded down in the byre where it was warm enough and private. Bess was thankful for an easy day after our long ride. The snow had fallen deeply leaving me unable to do much outside except work through a pile of wood cutting. I piled up some logs inside by the fire to dry and made sure there was a plentiful supply of fuel. I cleaned out the byre, laying down fresh bedding, and swept into corners that hadn't seen a broom in some time. The old horse barely moved and I thought better of trying to exercise it. An old nanny goat was equally stolid and my host barely raised a cupful when he milked it. Inside I built up the fire and swung the cauldron round towards the heat. I half-filled it with water and added chopped up turnip, some cabbage leaves and a handful of oatmeal, "That will thicken it up," but the old man who had barely moved throughout my whole visit, just stared at me. "Keep stirring it," I said, more to break the silence than anything else.

On the following morning, after I had saddled up to leave, I handed over the bread, cheese and pork fat to my host who nodded and said, "I don't know what you are running away from, but there's a place here for a young man like you." Running away? I said nothing. "We're not long for this world, my father and I. The place would be yours."

I briefly tried to picture the place in summer with some sheep in the top field. Build on to that byre, I thought, and make a paddock for horses; some cows for a proper milk supply and grow vegetables for market.

But then I thought of their Robbie wherever he may be or whatever he was doing, and again, I said nothing. It was the same old dream.

"I may be an old man, and I don't know what your business is in Carlisle, but I can judge a character and you're fine by me." This was as long a speech as any he'd made over the last two days. I leaned over to take the hand he offered. "May you ride with God's blessing."

"Thank-you," I said, knowing that no-one was more in need of God's blessing. I pushed Bess on to kick through the snow and find our way back to the road and the border.

Beneath a yellow sky, the lying snow cast an unnatural light over the land. It should have been beautiful but this was a desolate place where thuggery had ruled for hundreds of years. I had no wish to extend my time there. Progress was slow but I could not push for greater effort from Bess. I had stowed handfuls of feed for her and I passed it on sparingly mixing it with encouragement, "Good girl, good girl." And we crossed bitter rivers and passed villages and towns, deserted it would seem in the face of the unseasonal snow. There were times when I dismounted and led Bess by the reins over uneven ground; treachery would not be our undoing just yet. Our only course was to persevere and endure. So, when we arrived on the rim of a great bank overlooking a river bridge, a sombre castle and a cathedral beyond, I knew we had crossed the border and we were looking down over the city of Carlisle.

If this was one of the fine cities the English were building, I feared that Joseph had been misled. Even set within the white surrounds, it was grey and forbidding.

Dismal flags hung from both the castle and the cathedral and a few wisps of smoke drifted into the lowering sky. I had left Black Scaur Farm, a place of pestilent air, now I had arrived at a city of grim foreboding. I stood and thought long and hard but there was little option now, it couldn't have been much past noon but the November light was closing in and we had to make our move.

We dropped down towards the bridge crossing the river and advanced towards the gate in the city walls without being challenged. A group of sullen young men watched our approach but didn't alter their lazy postures, huddled as they were against the wall. They were armed though. I made a point of not looking too closely, but one carried a Lochaber axe and another a broken sword. All of them were poorly dressed with little defence against the November cold, but they had their weapons and maybe it was this that gave them their cocksure air. The leading one of these men did step across our path as I approached the gate.

"Are you looking to serve?"

I barely understood what he said but I had no wish to prolong our conversation. "I have business at the castle."

In truth, I had little desire to go the castle, it had the most dismal appearance of this God-forsaken city, but I was banking on the castle having stables and horses and somewhere I could find shelter and rest for Bess. But now the other men were picking up their slovenly postures, gathering like hungry dogs at the prospect of food.

"And what business would that be?"

"The business to which I have to attend."

"And our business is to keep an eye open for spies." He turned and smirked to his mates. "Are you a spy? Are you armed?"

1 1

"I'm not a spy." I could be adamant in my denial on that score, but I carried my dirk in amongst the pleats of my plaid.

"Get down off the horse. We need to do a search."

The men were closing in now, sensing at least a bit of late in the day fun but I could not consent to a search.

"I shall do no such thing."

"Well, in that case we'll have to get you down."

I tugged sharply on Bess's reins and made her rear. The men retreated but it only bought me a little time as they circled again keeping a wary eye on Bess's hooves. Their ill-assortment of weapons was raised and the leading man made a grab for Bess's halter. I leaned forward and swung as forceful a blow as I could muster, a wild swipe which missed its target. Unbalanced, I had no defence against a great clout which struck me on the shoulder from my blind side and dumped me on the slush-covered stone kerb. I gasped with the impact of landing but I knew I had to regain my feet quickly despite the pain which racked my ribcage. Winded, I had little response to my chief adversary who had dodged my swinging fist and was now making a grab at my plaid. I wriggled to evade his grasp but in trying to find my feet again, we both slipped and I was pinned back down on the kerb and he landed on top of me, his stinking breath reeking over my face. I was surely lost, for in that moment he knew. Confusion turned to realisation as the truth dawned and he was about to announce it to everyone else.

"Hey!"

But he could say no more.

"What is the meaning of this?" The sudden shout took us all by surprise. Without any of us noticing, a gentleman had appeared from the city side of the gate. "This is an outrage, and no way to treat a guest of mine!"

If the men were going to test this bluff, if that indeed is what it was, now was the time, they did not want their prize to slip away so easily, but his next words brought about their immediate compliance. "If I have a mind to tell the Duke of Perth, or indeed the Prince himself, you will have to bear the burden of these actions."

I rose to my feet reaching painfully for Bess's reins but I had trouble straightening, my right shoulder carried a dull ache from the blow I had taken and my left hip could barely hold my weight. But I knew that the well-dressed gentleman who had arrived out of nowhere, summoning indignation on my behalf, had been my saviour. The men slunk back against the wall of the gateway fearful of what they had brought upon themselves but the gentleman was now more concerned about my welfare. He offered his arm to me for assistance and together we led Bess to an inglorious entry into the city.

It wasn't difficult to find a quiet place. Few souls stirred and I soon knew the reason why as Doctor James Stratton made continual inquiries about my well-being.

"Instructions have been issued quite clearly: the citizens are to be left to go about their normal business without undue interference. Prince Charles himself gave out that order. Let me examine you, I am fearful of further damage."

But I could not allow that, insisting that I had suffered nothing worse than bruising although my limp was scant support for my claim.

"Joseph, you say. Are you a Hanoverian or a Jacobite, Joseph?"

This was a benighted place, not suited to frivolity but I sensed a light-heartedness in the Doctor's tone.

"My horse is neither Hanoverian nor Jacobite, but she will eat the feed of either. And I am of much the same opinion."

It was a long time since I heard such laughter and I felt some warmth in that I had been the source. He clapped me on the back, a friendly blow I could barely withstand, and he said, "Such a wise horse! We must, if we can, find some accommodation for you both. But tell me, Joseph, why have you arrived in Carlisle when almost everyone else, anyone able to, has left?"

Dr Stratton had proved to be my guardian angel at the north gate to the city, along with his humour, he had shown me a kindness which had long been absent. I told him my story and everything of which I spoke was true although I had to make major omissions.

"And you came to Carlisle because you thought the Jacobites would be in Newcastle?"

I nodded although I was well aware now that this was not the case. I had arrived in a city recently surrendered to rebels. He continued, "Well, I think it is time a little bit of Jacobite good fortune came your way. Don't go to the castle. If you are as good with horses as I think you are, you should go to Highmore House. It is kept by Mr Highmore himself. He won't see you this late in the day, but go to the stables and ask for Thomas. He's a good lad, not much older than yourself, I'm thinking, but he'll look after you. Take good care to tell him that you arrive with my recommendation: Dr James Stratton."

I would not forget the name, nor his generosity. I followed his directions without any further mishaps with the citizens or their recent captors, and before long, Bess and I stood before an imposing house, grander than anything I had been close to before. I knew I should make my way round the back and try and present myself to Thomas, but I stayed for a while imagining life in a house such as this.

"So, you think you're good with horses, eh? And Dr Stratton gives you a recommendation?" He looked at me as though doubtful. "Well, I reckon that's good enough for me." I knew I should have been grateful but I also knew he was still sizing me up. "There's not much meat on those bones though, is there?"

"I'm planning to lead the horses, not carry them."

"That so? Well, I tell you what, there's a spare stall for your horse, settle her down and give her some feed, then report back here. There's a couple of horses I want you to look at."

He *was* sizing me up and he was about to test me out. I'd spent most of the day riding, I'd had an encounter with some unruly Jacobites on sentry duty, I ached everywhere and I was done in for the day, but if Thomas Graham wanted to test me, then so be it. He had a lively air about him and he strode around those stables with the confidence of a man who knew his place. His business was horses and that suited me, let him test me as much as he wanted, I would meet any such challenge.

When I reported back to him, I knew he'd been watching me all along. He watched me unsaddle Bess, brush her down, place a blanket over her and then supply the water and feed she earned that day. "Well done, Bess. Well done. You've done us both proud today."

The two horses he wanted me to see were in a separate stable. He led me into the darkened stalls and pointed them out. One was a magnificent grey, although some would describe her as white, and the other was a skittish dun.

"So, what do you reckon to these two, Joe?"

They were both impressive animals although totally opposed in temperament.

"Let them out, can you? Walk the grey around the yard."

If Thomas thought I was being a little forward, he didn't object. He untied the horse and led her out of the stall, walked her around the yard two or three times and then returned her to the stall.

"And now the dun."

"Oh no, I've taken my turn. You lead her."

This then, was the challenge being laid down. Before I got anywhere near to untying her, she was whinnying and stamping. She was trying to lay down the law. I edged myself as far to the front of the stall as possible and approached her face on. I was in no hurry; I could take as long as she wanted.

"Now, what's the problem, eh? What's the problem?"

I talked softly to her, reaching up and brushing my hand down her nose. These were unsettling times and the horse had sensed it. It was time to talk and reassure.

"What a fine horse you are." I continued to stroke her nose and lead her out of the stall into the yard where she showed just how fine she was as I walked her

around the farthest edges of the yard. As for Thomas'
challenge, I reckon I met it well enough.

"Well done, Joe. She can be a right handful and you
made it look easy."

"They're both fine horses. Whose are they?"

"You don't know?" He laughed at me. "We are
entertaining some fine guests. These horses belong to
Prince Charles himself."

It was true, I knew very little but I didn't want to
confess my ignorance. I let Thomas tell me more about
Prince Charles and his army. They were marching to
London. They'd pulled a fast one over the King's army
which was stuck in Newcastle, unable to cross the
country because of the snow and ice. They were
marching to London because the Prince was going to
claim the crown for his father – the rightful king.

"I don't know how much longer they'll stay.
It's our job to look after the horses, so what d'ye
reckon?"

"They're both fine horses," I knew I was repeating
myself but I was much happier talking about horses
than marching on London. "The dun needs a lot of
attention. Let her see who cleans out her stall and
provides her feed. Talk to her while she's being brushed.
She's strong, very strong, but she'll soon respond and
serve her master well."

"And the grey?"

"Another fine horse, but she's exhausted and she's
carrying her back leg a little. Go easy on her for as
many days as you've got. Give her regular but small
feeds. Walking around the yard will be sufficient
exercise."

"Goodness, Joe, you know your horses."

If I thought we were finished for the day, I was wrong. We did all manner of sweeping and clearing, we tidied and organised tackle and long after the lamps in the stables had been lit, we worked to produce the finest yard in all England. We didn't stop until Thomas sensed it was time and a boy from the kitchen brought us some mutton pie and a hunk of bread. It was the most welcome supper I'd had in days.

"We'll be getting some hot water tonight." Thomas was finishing his pie. "We need a good wash after all of this. We've got blankets, we'll bed down over there."

It would be warm enough and comfortable in the stables, I had no doubt of that, but it wasn't that which concerned me. I needed privacy to wash and there was nowhere else I could go, no excuse I could use, I would just have to plead exhaustion myself and retire immediately.

For once, I didn't need to pretend. My whole body ached; my shoulder and hip were constant reminders of the welcome I had received in Carlisle. But as I crawled under my blanket, I realised how Thomas had added sweetness to my bitter reception. He was keen to show off his position as chief stable hand but he was generous in his acknowledgement of my contribution. He was building up both of us.

"A fine afternoon's work, Joe. The pair of us, a fine piece of work." And what's more, I glowed in his praise.

The water arrived in a relay of pails and it was poured into a half barrel. Thomas slipped out of his woollen jacket and breeches and his slender, white body and limber legs shone in the flickering dark of the stable. He cupped his hands together to dowse himself with the water then ducked his head in the barrel and pulled it out again making a great splash. Despite myself, I watched the rivulets of water run down his neck and spine to the hollow of his back and buttocks. In and out of the shadows, his muscular body, occasionally glimpsed like a majestic salmon forging through spray. He began pummelling himself with a woollen cloth and I turned over in my newly-made bed space and looked away before he finished this vigorous assault on his own body. I knew that Thomas had laid out his blankets on the straw next to mine and as soon as he had completed his wash and nipped the wicks in the lamps in the stable, he would be climbing into his bed no more than an arm's length from me.

I heard him pick his way around the stall we had adopted and felt the movement as he lay down and settled. There was a long period of deep breathing in the darkness until he broke the silence.

"Joe, are you still awake?" I didn't answer and didn't know why not. "Joe, Mr Highmore pays me and gives me my keep. I'm in charge of the horses here. What I say goes…" and then he paused as though he hadn't worked out what he was going to say next, "…and now you've arrived. We need your help. But it's my word that holds." Still not knowing what to say, I didn't answer and eventually he continued, "But I've a feeling that we shall be friends…great friends…and you should call me Tom."

I tried to control my breathing. I couldn't speak now because I knew that whatever it was that Tom was feeling, I felt it too. But what that meant for both of us, I could not say.

For the next two days we worked hard, rising before dawn and seeing to every task. Often, we worked together, sometimes we worked apart, but as often as I dared, I stole a look at Tom, commanding amongst the horses yet speaking softly, showing them the respect, they deserved. How I admired his authority and balance and how I wanted to confide in him. When the meals arrived from Mr Highmore's fine kitchen, we would sit together and tear up chunks of bread. Between mouthfuls, Tom would praise me and then tease me.

"More splendid work from you Joe. I reckon you were born to be a stableman. Get some of this bread inside you though, and this cheese. We have to build you up. Stables are no place for la'al sparrers." His eyes shone as he looked to me for a response but I couldn't find the words. How could I tell him that these were days I would never forget?

Nor would I forget how they came to an end. We were sweeping out the stables when I became aware of a small company of men standing at the doorway. When I looked up, I was startled by the appearance of the gentleman who stood right at the centre of the group. He looked like no other man I had ever seen. That he was strikingly handsome was obvious, his very air seemed to attract all attention to him. He wore a blue bonnet and a tartan plaid with a broad belt over his left shoulder ornamented with a rosette. He had a star on his left breast and his hair was secured with a ribbon. I knew well enough who this man was and understood why many women were reported to be in thrall to Prince Charles. The men around him too, paid great attention to every word he said.

"We must issue and immediate order: do not eat the babies of the local people."

It brought a round of laughter from the men. The locals' fear of the barbaric Highlanders was not well-founded. The courtesy of the rebels had been exemplified by their leader and, as he spoke again, it was obvious that the French inflection to his voice only added more to his appeal.

"Now, where are these stable hands who have done such sterling work with our horses?"

"Sir?" Tom stepped forward.

"Thomas, is it not?"

"Yes, Sir."

"We are well pleased. Do not think your work will go unrewarded."

"Thank you, Sir. If I may say so, sir, I have not worked alone. I have received considerable assistance from Joseph."

I had sought to stay in the shadows during this meeting but I was alarmed now to be pushed forward.

"And this, I take it, is Joseph." I half expected the usual comment about my lack of size, some disbelief about my ability to work amongst these magnificent creatures, but the Prince had more serious intent. "Joseph, reports of your work travel before you and now we are here to take your advice."

For the first time I looked in earnest at the men surrounding the Prince and noticed that Dr Stratton was among their number and I was gratified by his wink and nod of encouragement.

"We march tomorrow," the Prince continued, "and I need advice on which of my horses to ride. What do you say, Joseph, the grey or the dun?"

If I had been fearful in the presence of the Prince and these men, such fear was allayed now. If he wanted to talk about horses then I was perfectly content.

"Sir, the grey is a strong horse, solid and reliable. The dun has more spirit but both will serve you well."

"But your final answer, Joseph. Not even my most devoted followers will believe that I can ride two horses at once." This drew muted laughter from the men which was soon halted because the Prince sought an answer. "So, for spirit, I should take the dun?"

"No, sir." There was no chance of any laughter now. I had just contradicted the Prince and the recent favour I had won now stood to be lost. "Sir, I don't believe that either horse will let you down but your choice should be to ride the grey."

"The grey?"

"There is nothing to choose between these two horses now but their appearance. We know this horse to be grey but in the popular telling of your story you will be the Prince who rode a white horse."

The sudden silence which fell over the stable suggested that my gift for impertinence had resurfaced. The Prince stepped forward and placed both of his hands on my shoulders.

"Wisdom beyond your years." He stroked my cheek. "Seventeen, they tell me, and not yet shaving. Joseph, what do you say to riding with us to London tomorrow? Take charge of my horses and I will pay you well."

I hesitated and my hesitation was obvious. March to London alongside the Prince, stay here in Carlisle where I had found a happiness I had never experienced before or answer the call to return to Black Scaur Farm?

I was being presented with a crossroads between desire and duty.

"Are you with us Joseph? Are you a supporter of the cause?"

The silence concentrated upon me. The Prince, whose command should not be resisted, his chief advisers ready to jump as ordered, and Tom, wonderful, wonderful, Tom, all waited for my answer. I had to speak.

"I must thank you for your offer, Sir, it is not a position I had ever dreamed of, but I must respectfully decline. I support anyone doing the right thing by their father and it is *that* which calls me back to Scotland."

No-one spoke or moved before the Prince's reaction. He tightened his grip around my shoulders and any levity now dropped from his voice, "A sound answer but one I regret. Go well, Joseph, go well. You have our thanks for your service."

He'd understood all too well the importance of appearances. The Prince on a white horse would serve him well as a story, but I could no longer live with the deception I'd created. It would be three years yet until I reached seventeen, and no, I was not shaving, but I was binding myself, and for these last six months, I had been bleeding.

Just as surely as the Prince's lay in London, my destiny and any redemption I could salvage was held in Black Scaur Farm. He sought justice for his father, I had to make my peace with the dreadful events of that night when I had lain awake through the long hours.

Another night of degradation when I had lain awake listening to the grunting and snoring until I knew it was time. I had evaded the desperate grasping, calculating the hours remaining until dawn. It had been a tortuous night but eventually, I convinced myself that it was time.

I edged myself out of the bed away from the deep rattling and muttering. Every disturbance urged further caution on my part. He must not wake now.

I could dress in the dark, I had done it many times, fastening my shirt at the neck and cuffs. I was going to need my belted plaid for warmth and I could hide beneath its pleats. I was silent, moving with stealth among the shadows. I checked the bag on my belt which held the small amount of money I had gleaned and the length of woollen cloth I would need. But I could go no further without a flicker of light. I slipped across to the fireplace and blew on the ash, and then blew again to nurture a glow. There, just the merest inkling and that was enough to trail in a taper and let it catch. Better, much better. I could now be certain about where I was going and what I was doing. I stepped back towards the bed and the outlined figure of the grunting beast, I was feeling for my dirk. Now, now was the time to act. But my feet would move no further and my nerve was failing. With a taper in one hand and a dirk in the other I stood over the heaving mound hesitating. The body before me gave a sudden roar and heaved itself into a new position. He was waking surely, and I was undone. But no, he lurched back towards a deeper sleep and I regained my breath. His new position, lying on his back with throat vibrating had made my task easier. I had to move now, I had to act so I stepped forward further still and drew back the woollen blanket revealing the coarse beard, the thick neck and the barrelled chest, rising and falling in great respirations. I placed the point of my dirk on his shirt feeling for a gap between his ribs.

There, that was the very spot. My dirk was at the ready and our souls were teetering over the abyss when his eyelids opened and he fixed his eyes on mine.

That moment of dull incomprehension between sleep and waking. What? Why? I could delay no longer, panic propelled me and I thrust the dirk in between the ribs, deep into his heart and like an old boar being stuck he made one more grunt and then gave up the unequal struggle between life and death. The desperate wheezing ceased and his last grasp lessened. I stood waiting until I was sure, then pulled out the dirk, sliding it out of the black gore that had pooled over his shirt and bedclothes. Then I stepped back and stared at the sight which would haunt me all my living days. The sight that would prompt my prayers. Forgive me, forgive me Father.

Calmness, Courage and Duty

The day that Miss James was shown into the front room to sip tea out of the best china cups was also the day that I nearly drowned.

"Go and fetch your brother."

My mother was referring to my brother Paul, two years my junior, not William or George, who both worked on the railway and wouldn't brook any fetching from me. And because we spent so much time together, except for when he was at school, she always assumed that I knew where Paul would be, and she was right. The choice was always the woods, the rabbit warren or the river. The woods, as the light faded in the evening, was a better bet; the best time for setting and checking snares, and the best time for waiting and watching. Paul knew where all the birds nested and where the badgers would emerge from their sett. He knew where the foxes' dens were, and when vixens were likely to move their cubs. He knew about stealth and about the importance of making approaches from downwind; observing and stalking. He knew about these things because that's what I'd taught him.

"Go and fetch your brother."

But at that time of day, I knew he'd be down at the river and I also knew why Mam wanted to speak to him. If stealth around animals is useful, around grownups it's vital. Make yourself silent, make yourself invisible and see where that gets you. For me, it made me privy to a lot of conversations and I knew why Miss James had been taken into the front room to drink tea from the best china cups.

The river was our malign neighbour. Still long and languid after a lazy summer, the river had a fascination for us both. We knew of its threat, but always it had the allure of potential treasure. Paul would be down there now finding the best position, making sure that the sun was not casting treacherous shadows. I had to close my eyes to a squint, to pick him out in his favourite spot, bent double up to his knees in the river flow, poised like a heron.

On the riverside path, I increased my speed taking care to make a silent approach. I was less than twenty yards away from him when he darted, a hand movement quicker than a pike. A hit! But then he was struggling to stand upright again and he slipped and disappeared below the surface of the water. His head emerged and then was lost again into the increasing depths. Now I ran flat out. He wasn't far from the bank but there was nothing I could chuck out for him to grab. I may have gasped at the shock of cold water but I plunged straight in, not understanding why Paul's attempts to save himself should be so hampered. My only thought was to get a hold of something and drag him clear of the dark god of the undercurrent. But there wasn't a flailing arm I could clutch, both arms were wrapped around his chest as though he had consigned himself to this fate. So, instead, I got a handful of sodden hair and put my other hand around the back of his neck and began to pull, only to lose my own footing and slide, still with my clamp grip on Paul, into the wild silence below the surface.

And then back clear again, gulping a lungful of air before another descent and a remorseless drag downstream. We were pulled, buffeted and tossed around before finally being discarded; eddied into a shallow and a last chance we couldn't scorn, from here we could reach the river's muddy edge, and together in our desperate embrace we scrambled and staggered towards the bank heaving and exhausted.

Did I get him out or did he pull me on to the grassy sanctuary? I don't remember. I couldn't think; I was curled up in agony as though someone had run a giant stitch through my upper body and was now pulling it tight. Then there was the coughing, the pain in my chest and my conviction that now, it was my turn to take a two-step with death.

I don't know how long I lay on that bank waiting for peace. It was not to be, not yet. I finally turned myself agonisingly onto my elbow to find that the river was still flowing, the wind still blew and the tall grass was singing. I was alive, and Paul, who wouldn't have been the first to be charmed and swallowed by those depths, was crouched on all fours beside me, wretched, drenched and smiling.

"Blasted fish," he said, "nearly did for us both."

And lying beside him was the magnificent salmon wrestled from the river which had now breathed its last.

We ducked through hedges and nipped across fields on the way back to the house. "Has she gone then?"

He'd taken off his jumper to try and cover his booty from the river. I knew Paul was talking about Miss James and I nodded.

"And was she on about the Grammar School and sitting for a scholarship?"

I nodded again and Paul sighed.

"She said as much to me at school. She'll give me extra tuition she says."

It was the burden Paul felt he had to carry. How ever it was that these things were decided, he'd been given brains. William and George had been granted fine upright physiques and had been deemed suitable for jobs on the railway, while I spent my prescribed time roaming wild amongst the fields and fells on the notion that fresh air was what I needed. I knew Paul would do anything to swap places with me; the tyranny of books and the cage of the classroom in exchange for my freedom. But what he didn't know was that I would gladly swap in return.

"I bet Mam was all for it, wasn't she?"

Maybe she was, but it wasn't as straightforward as that. She wanted the best for Paul, yes, and this was a marvellous opportunity, but she kept talking about the uncertainty of the times, about who knew what tomorrow would bring. And Miss James had nodded gravely, handling the delicate china before she said that there were some things that neither she nor Mam could affect, the world rolled on one way or another.

"All I can do," she said, "is teach, and all Paul can do, is take full advantage of his gifts."

Mam had nodded in return, she wasn't going to disagree but she ended the conversation by saying,

"Of course, it is my husband who will make the final decision."

"Of course."

And I knew what that meant.

Mam took one look at us on our dripping, muddy return and sprang into an immediate response. She grabbed either side of my head and looked into my eyes.

"Are you alright?" She turned to Paul, "Is he alright? Has he coughed? Blood?" She flared. "What on earth where you thinking about?"

"He jumped in after me, Mam. He pulled me out."

That she had two hands still on my head was a good thing. It meant she wasn't going to clout me.

"Get yourselves out of these wet things. There's nothing else for it, you'll have to put on your Sunday best. I'll wrap this..." she indicated the salmon which lay blank-eyed on the table "in some newspaper and you can take it round to the Crown. Use the back door and ask for Mr Bishop in the kitchen."

We were set on our way with strict instructions. "Make sure he knows who you are and get a fair price."

And we marched off with Paul, carrying his prize catch wrapped in newspaper, setting a confident pace. What did she mean by that? Did Paul know who we were, and what did she think would be a fair price?

When he was called to the kitchen door, Mr Bishop's look of annoyance soon dropped when he caught sight of what Paul was carrying and he ushered us in out of the broad daylight. He took the parcel from Paul and unfolded the newspaper away from the fish.

"And I suppose you'll be wanting some money for this?"

"My Mam says to get a fair price," said Paul.

"Did she now? I wonder if her idea of a fair price is the same as mine?"

Undeterred, Paul continued, "she says to make sure you know who we are."

Mr Bishop gave us a long hard look before he replied,

"Oh, I know who you are alright. You're Grahams, two of the station master's lads. And your mother is Mary Graham. But I know her from years ago when she was Mary Small from Inkerman Terrace."

"I'm Paul and this is Davy. Davy doesn't speak."

Mr Bishop gave a quick look at me and then continued, "Well, hasn't she done well, Mary Small from Inkerman Terrace? Married to the station master with two strapping lads and another one who's a bright lad at school, or so I hear."

He turned and gave another look at me and said no more. Like a lot of people, he probably thought I was deaf.

"Well, we'd better get this straightened out. It's a fine fish and I'll pay a fair price. Hold out your hand."

He dug into his trouser pocket, pulled out a handful of coins and placed some onto Paul's outstretched hand. Paul did not take his eyes off the big chef but I'm sure he was totalling up each of the coins in turn, and when Mr Bishop finished, Paul did not close his fist.

"What?" The big man did not look pleased.

Paul didn't flinch, he just said as a matter of fact, "It nearly killed both of us, pulling that fish out of the river."

It was difficult to tell whether Mr Bishop was about to lose his temper or whether he was mildly amused, but his big white apron and the towel he had tucked into his waistband said that he was a busy man and we were taking up his time. He bent down towards Paul and lowered his voice.

"Listen, you might be a bright lad, but don't go telling anyone about pulling a fish out of that river. Understand?" Paul nodded, but he hadn't yet closed his fingers around those coins and Mr Bishop realised that he would have to continue. "You're a good negotiator though, I'll give you that. You should have been with Mr Chamberlain in Berlin, eh?" He gave out a bitter laugh before directing his attention back to Paul. "Put that money in your pocket. It's a fair price for your mother. But this is to seal the deal. One for you and one for your brother."

I dodged his wink and looked at the shiny sixpence he had just pressed into my hand. "Now, if you "find" any more fish, you know where to come. And the way things are going, I can only see the price going up."

By the time we got outside and began our walk home, the coin – a fortune to me – was inside my trouser pocket burning against my thigh. I looked across at Paul and he looked back.

"No, I've no idea what that was all about, but I do know that we've got a little secret now, haven't we?"

That tiny coin inside my pocket felt as big as a millstone. He was going to keep that sixpence? We were both going to keep our sixpences? I couldn't chase this thought much further. A shrill blast from a train pierced the early evening calm.

"That'll be the tea time goods going through. He'll be home soon," said Paul, and we both quickened our step.

We were back home first and Paul pushed over the coins that Mr Bishop had given him. Mam counted them and then looked steadily at both of us in turn.

"And it was Mr Bishop you saw?" I found a speck of dirt to clear from my Sunday best trousers before she continued, "Well, you'd better get your hands washed and be ready for your brothers and father coming home for tea."

William and George followed soon after, striding into the house with confident smiles. They had done a week's work; they were contributing, and on a Saturday night they would be going dancing. But a silence fell over us all as we heard the unmistakable irregular thud of Father negotiating his way through the door and barging into the hallway.

When we were all settled around the table, Father said grace. *May we all be suitably grateful,* and then we could make a start. We had cold tongue with a boiled egg and potatoes. In the middle of the table was a plate piled with buttered sliced bread. Except we didn't make a start because with a sudden rush, Father pushed back his chair and used his arms to lever himself upright. Then, with his well-practiced heavy hop, he pounded over to the cutlery drawer, picked up a knife and then pounded back again.

"I'd have thought," he grumbled, "with four sons in the house, I wouldn't have to fetch my own knife."

His insistence that the house should run with the same smoothness as his milk train and two freight trains a day, branch line railway station, had been broken.

It was left to William, my oldest brother to answer. "Father, if any one of us had realised that you were without a knife, I'm sure we would gladly have got one for you."

Father didn't reply and Mam gave an almost imperceptible nod of approval at this crisis being averted.

There was no breakfast on Sunday before we accepted the Sacrament. We made our weekly visit to church to celebrate our faith and cement our status. It was at church, at the gathering on the way in and the mingling on the way out, that I found out who we were. My tendency to meld into crowds of adults often paid dividends. The Graham family from Railway House; we were respected and resented.

"She might well look pleased with herself. Marriage brought her three fine sons and a big house."

"Four sons."

"Aye, three fine sons and the dumb one."

"But she kept her word and stayed by him when he came back from France."

"She was a lucky one. There's many that didn't get chance to keep their word; their men didn't come back."

"The William Graham that I knew went to France as a handsome young man. Always had a cheerful word for everyone. It wasn't the William Graham that came back."

"No, he left more than a leg in France."

We had our own pew in church by custom and practice more than anything else. Third from the front on the right-hand side. We even sat in rank order and I was at the end next to Paul, both of us polished and brushed and warned to be on our best behaviour. It was always a long hour and a half in prospect. Only that morning was different. It was a much shorter service than usual adding to the peculiarity of the day and the strange mood which infected all of the church attenders. The vicar gathered his cassock and surplice and climbed up to his delivery point in the pulpit to surprise us all.

"There is nothing I can say to you this morning except to say that you should all take the opportunity to examine your conscience before God."

He couldn't know, surely, that one of his congregation sat with an illicitly gained sixpence secreted in his trouser pocket?

"The time will come shortly for each and every one of us to do our duty. God will protect the righteous, He will always take the side of the faithful." The vicar paused as if to give everyone the opportunity to start examining their consciences there and then. "Now, I suggest that we make a peaceful departure. Go home and listen to the Prime Minister on the radio and may God bless you all."

It should have been a blessing in itself that we had got out of church early but there would be no escape into the fields. A mood of dread anticipation had fallen.

We all gathered in the front room to listen to the radio, the same front room where only a day earlier, Miss James had been advocating a Grammar School future for Paul. In the solemn room which was normally kept for best, we gathered under the gaze of those animal pictures: the magnificent stag and the skewered otter being held above the hounds. I thought we would be standing to listen to this broadcast, but while the radio was warming up, Father sat down in the tall armchair and perched his crutches alongside. So, we all sat, filling up the huge sofa and the additional two armchairs and no-one spoke.

Eventually, the crackling from the speaker ceased and a voice emerged loud and clear. It was the clipped tones of Mr Chamberlain, the Prime Minister, speaking to us, he said, from the Cabinet Room in 10 Downing Street. It was all about the British Ambassador in Berlin handing a final note to the German government. He was building up the detail; the note, a deadline and troops in Poland, until eventually he made the statement: "…consequently this country is at war with Germany." And my mother, my solid, dependable mother, gasped and slumped while my elder brothers sat up and stiffened.

Mr Chamberlain continued, talking about Hitler and how unreliable he was, he talked about how he now needed to be stopped by force. He talked about brave resistance, of calmness and courage and when he finished, Father said quite simply, "Switch it off, William."

And once again silence swept in around the room until William, standing, to attention, said, "Tomorrow morning, I shall go and enlist."

Before anyone could respond, George said, "And I shall do likewise."

Mam looked across at Father who was saying nothing so she spoke herself, "William, you've got a job on the railway. You'll be doing your war work here. George, you're too young."

"I'll tell them I'm eighteen."

"Don't be ridiculous." I'd never seen Mam so agitated, "You work on the railway as well."

"They'll take me, I know they will."

"For King and Country, Mother." William spoke again. "We have to do our duty."

"Duty!" Mam blazed. "Your father did his duty in the last lot and look where that got him." She turned towards Father. "William, you were in France. Tell them what it was like in France doing your duty for King and Country!"

Everyone's eyes turned towards Father who, as far as I knew, had never spoken about France. He adjusted his sitting position causing his crutches to slide down the arm of the chair and crash to the floor; a clatter which he ignored. He looked anguished, caught between head and heart, he could only stare bleakly into the middle distance. Finally, he broke the awful silence.

"They will find it more honourable to sign up than to stay at home."

That was it, Mam's two eldest sons were pulling away and the man she called husband was waving a flag. Bereft, she could only play the last card she had in her hand,

"They also serve who sit at home and wait."

It was something she'd read from some writer somewhere, and as soon as she said it, I knew Paul would be sitting an examination for his scholarship. The world of books would not be denied her son.

Almost as if the thought had entered her mind, she turned to Paul. "And you, Paul, how old are you?"

"Ten, Mam."

"How many years is it until you can go and lie about your age?"

With that, she rose to her feet and barged out of the

room leaving the men in her life to contemplate honour and courage.

No-one had included me in the sudden plans for war, but I knew where my duty lay. I needed to follow my mother and clear my conscience.

She was in the kitchen holding on to the back of a chair as if to keep herself upright. It was a wild and frightened look she gave which pierced me to the core, but I would do what I had to do. I reached into my pocket and withdrew my hand with the sixpence laid out across my outstretched palm. I walked towards her proffering the coin to which she gave a long hard stare before fixing her gaze on me with beseeching eyes. Now, now would be the time and I fought to do that for which she longed. It was a fight where rage and frustration battled deep within my soul, but no sound came and silence continued to reign in the normally busy hive of the kitchen. Slowly, I saw realisation creep into her eyes. There would be no victory here until I could scale the barricade before me. I flinched from my mother's look while she took each of my fingers in turn, folded them over the gleaming sixpence and then squeezed my dwarfed fist.

"Oh, Davy, Davy" She was hugging my head suffocatingly close to her breast now, "Calmness and courage? That man... Men... they don't know the half of it, do they?"

Touching the Honey Slow River

Downstream from the textiles factory where the current ran thick with effluent dyes of vivid reds, violets and blues was the favoured spot. Always, there was a thick scum of sullied foam which would catch in high wind and float in perverse clouds above the surface of the water. It was dirty and dangerous and we were told never to go down there. But forbidden fruit never looked so sweet and the Honey Slow River sucked us in.

It was during the long weeks of summer when we clambered down through the rampant elders and gorse to the patch of dried mud which we fancied as sand. Down to the Dingle. Here status was accorded to position, the low branches or the exposed tree roots, but the rule remained inviolable, the best positions were held by the hardest kids. I kept to the fringes, keen to pick up what these boys knew, keen not to expose my younger status and face ignominious expulsion. I was hanging out with Tommo, Badger, Wilf and Danny, hoping one day for a nickname myself as a proclamation.

There, where the river lay alongside us in torpor, occasionally flicking a tongue or blinking a malignant eye, we pronounced on things we knew to be true. The news was full of world conflict but if another war was to be declared, our country would win easily even if it was against the Russians or the Chinese and there were millions of them. My uncle fought against the Chinese in Korea, said one boy keen to claim approbation but who then let his voice fade away. The next war will be a nuclear war, said another. Who would win that? Sometimes reassurance was elusive and it was better to turn to subjects about which we feared no contradiction. Like that lass that was pulled out of the river a few years ago.

Three days she was in the river before they pulled her out.

A week!

No, it was longer than that.

And her condition was also ripe for speculation: bloated features with the body full of river water, distended eyeballs and her flesh eaten by fish and other stuff. No-one could claim a relative working for the police or the coroner, so there was no trump card to be laid in this discussion and we let our gory imaginations roam.

"Which lasses would you like to get down here?"

A list of names was suggested during which time I said nothing. It was only through distant fame or notoriety that I knew the names of these girls who were older than I was and I noticed others too, holding back, making sure that whatever they said would fit with the prevailing opinion.

It was a rough-looking boy sitting on one of the most favoured tree stumps who spat on the ground before him and said,

"You could get 'em down here... and do...anything."

And another silence fell as we all toyed with the dreadful delight of what he had just said. A silence that wasn't broken until someone called out,

"What about Lucy Loose?"

"Yeah!"

It was a popular call and the mood was restored.

"Yeah, Lucy Loose would show you her diamond."

"A diamond! Has she really got a diamond?"

They all turned to look and heap their scornful responses on me.

"Of course, she's got a diamond."

I tried to deflect the attention my comment had brought. Of course, she's got a diamond and of course I knew that. Someone suggested that Lucy Loose should put the diamond in her mouth to plug the gap in her teeth. Again, it won a round of uncertain laughter.

Sometimes there would be no-one down at the Dingle at all. The days stretched out like a fellside view when there was nowt to do, and the boredom was compounded when no-one else was knocking about. Like that languid summer afternoon. But the empty Dingle gave me the opportunity to try out all of the sitting positions. I climbed into the lower branches of a tree, the one from where all of the leadership commands were issued, and I liked it. It gave me an elevated view across part of the stagnant river and I could feel authority running through me. I could do this, sit and pass judgement on teachers at school, explain how we would sort out the Germans and the Japs if they started again or I could assume temporal knowledge when it came to lasses and what to do with them.

My leadership reverie was broken by the sound of someone approaching, someone pushing past the gorse bushes and slipping down the bank. It was someone alone. I hesitated, not wanting to call out or betray my presumptuous position until I knew the identity of this new arrival. I waited until the scraggy bushes parted and then, even with a partial view, thanks to descriptions I had picked up earlier, I knew who it was alright. Dirty blonde hair, that was one giveaway. "Hey," I called before attempting an elegant dismount from the tree branch. I was aiming to be as lithe as Robin Hood but I toppled over on landing, stamping my foot through the crust of mud into the wet clart below before standing up to try and regain some composure.

"Who are you?" The newcomer spoke before I did.

"I know who you are." I said, still intoxicated with my earlier vision of myself as a leader.

"Yeah, well who am I?"

"You're Lucy Loose."

"No-one calls me that."

Now that I had landed down at her level, I suddenly realised how big she was. Frighteningly big with bulging arms showing below her short-sleeved shirt, big enough to beat me in a fight. I could feel my former prestige dwindling. There was the large gap between her front teeth but I didn't dare stare.

"It's Lucy, just Lucy. Where is everyone?"

"I dunno."

"So, what are you doing down here?"

"Nowt, really. Just hangin' about. Nowt to do."

"So, what should we do?"

Lucy was attracting and repelling me. With her physical presence she filled the Dingle and when she smiled, she looked as though she was about to fasten her teeth into my neck. But she also had a clumsy mystique, hints of knowledge beyond footballers or wars, and when she talked to me, I didn't feel that she was always trying to get one over me.

"Well, any ideas?"

"Everyone reckons you've got a diamond."

"A diamond!" She laughed.

"Well, have you?"

"You don't know much, do you?" She was still laughing. "I might have. What have you got?"

I was at a loss. I had an old coffee tin full of marbles but I wasn't going to tell her that, she was already laughing, laughing and moving towards me, closing the space between us.

"Have you really got a snake?"

We were within touching distance now and she grabbed the metal clasp on the elasticated belt to my trousers.

"Your snake for my diamond. Wadd'ya say?"

This moment wasn't lost on me. I was on the verge of a story I would be able to tell all of the lads. I could climb to the higher branches with my story of what I did at the Dingle with Lucy Loose. But I was being gripped at the waistband by this overpowering girl and with a sudden sickness I realised that I was no longer in control and I didn't want this story, whatever it was going to be, to happen. There was the shameful certainty that I was trying not to cry and she suddenly let go.

"Are you okay?"

"Yeah, sure."

"I'm sorry, I was only kiddin' you." She was looking at me strangely now but I still wanted to cry. "You're okay you are. You're rubbish at getting' out of trees, but you're alright... Losemore, Lucy Losemore. That's my name."

When she smiled her gap-toothed smile, I decided I would never call her Lucy Loose again. She'd said I was alright. And so was she.

"I have to go anyway." I told her.

"You don't have to. We could hang about."

Apart from her smile there was something about Lucy that I liked. She was no longer bristling and her face had a kind of eager gleam. I wondered if you could be mates with a girl. We could do that thing about seeing who could chuck a stick furthest into the river.

"Nah, I have to go. I have to go into town with my mam."

Once I was clear of the Dingle and out in the open, I wanted to give out a great yell. I was ready to run home, galloping my horse like the Lone Ranger, dismissing baddies with silver bullets from my Colt 45. But it was not to be. I rounded a bend straight into a bunch of lads, older lads I didn't know who had strayed from their own patch. There were no preliminaries, no verbal jousting, I was immediately put into a headlock by the leader and bent double at the waist. I could see only the rough ground below me and his scuffed shoes.

"Gerroff!"

I grunted from my undignified position. It was hurting but I couldn't put much effort into breaking the hold for fear of an escalated reprisal. I was just trying to avoid total humiliation pinned as I was against the hip of my assailant trying to maintain my breathing through the grip of his headlock.

"What have we got here then?"

"Gerroff!" I said again.

"You wanna fight?" He was lording it, showing off his power and toying with me.

"No, just gerroff!"

"Why should I?"

I racked my brains for an answer.

"Because I know stuff."

"Yeah, what kind of stuff?"

I had one desperate gambit and I wasn't going to use it without some sort of concession from this lad.

"Gerroff an' I'll tell you."

"Okay then."

The headlock was released and I stood up to regain my breath as the lads moved in to hear what I had to say. If it wasn't good enough, I'd be back in the headlock and worse.

"Well...?"

I'd paused as long as I could. If I held back any longer, or if I didn't produce the goods...

"Lucy Loose is down there."

"Lucy Loose? Where?"

"Down there. Down in the Dingle." The boys looked speculatively towards the gap in the trees which led down to the Dingle. "And she's looking for some mates to hang about with." It was the craven embellishment which would haunt me for years but it achieved its short-term goal. Without a further word the boys trooped off down the path like a gang of malevolent monkeys. And I turned for home, no longer intent upon leaping up on to Silver and galloping like a hero, nor did I want to think about what I had just done. I trudged towards our house sick to the soles of my feet.

I must have been doing a poor job of hiding my feelings. I was walking down our back lane where Sam was sitting on his back step having a cigarette.

"Had a rough day, Young 'Un?"

Sam should have been everything my dad despised. He didn't work, he just spent every fine day sitting out the back smoking and watching the world go by.

Most people called him Loony Sam, some whispered about Burma and the railway, but Dad said, in that mysterious code of adults, that I should respect him on account of what he had seen.

"Yes, Mr Barber."

"Have a seat." He beckoned me to the space on the step next to him and I sat down. Together we sat and watched nothing happen. He continued to puff at his cigarette as the final hooter at the engineering works sounded and we heard a goods train rumbling down the track before he eventually spoke again. "You going to your new school soon?" It was true, when these holidays finally drew to a close, I would be going to the Grammar School. "There'll be rough days for you there as well." Which wasn't really what I wanted to hear. Expectation was already laying landmines around the notion of Grammar School. "Make the most of it though lad. There's not many from round here that goes to that school. Take your chances. You'll be doing homework soon not messing around at that river."

The fallacy that the Dingle was our secret place was well and truly exposed. Everyone knew everything about everywhere and everyone else around our way. News travels fast and scandal even faster. I woke up the following morning to the sound of raised voices in our back kitchen. Instinct told me to stay upstairs but I pulled on some clothes and went down to see what it was all about.

Dad was blazing. He rarely shouts but for this he was raging.

"Were you at that bloody river yesterday?" I'd never heard him swear either but something or someone had well and truly lit his blue touch paper. Red-faced, there was thunder behind his eyes. He bent down and picked up my shoes with an incriminating tide mark of mud lapping over the soles onto the uppers. "Well, were you at that bloody river?"

A night's sleep should have banished all of the events of the previous day, but no, what I had done and what I had failed to do was posted before me in the shape of my muddy shoes.

"I went looking for everyone. I was looking for someone...to play with."

Even in my defensive state I realised how tame that last phrase sounded.

"You went to the river! After everything we've told you, you went to the river? What did you do there?"

"Nothing, there was nobody there. I came away again."

"What time was that?"

"I dunno, early. I was talking to Sa...Mr Barber... Tea-time!" I suddenly remembered. "Spender's hooter sounded while I was sitting on Mr Barber's step."

An impasse and the rage looked like abating. Mam, who had been standing in a darkened corner of the kitchen stepped forward. I decided to offer a pawn to hostage. "Mr Barber asked me if I wanted a cigarette." But I was ignored. Mam pulled on Dad's arm.

"You see, he wasn't there, Jack. He wasn't there at the time they're talking about."

Dad looked at me with the strangest look I have ever seen. Thinking about it now, there was dissipating anger, worry, relief and, although I would never have known it then, something else, love, yes, that's what it was, love. He spoke more quietly,

"Go back to your room. We've told you many a time not to go to that river. Go back to your room and don't move. I'll speak to you later."

I left the kitchen with the practised skill of not closing the door hard enough. Ajar, if I walked slowly, I'd hear the next words spoken.

"Oh, thank God for that Jack. But that poor girl, the poor bairn."

Images of Lucy passed before my eyes as I shuffled back up the stairs, water-bloated Lucy. Lucy with her eyes distended in death being pulled out of the Honey Slow River.

I kept well clear of the river after that and I didn't see much of Tommo, Badger and the rest of the gang. We were bound on separate courses. I started at the Grammar School where the Headmaster told us that one day, we would become leaders in our small town, leaders in business and in the way the town was run. Our careers might even take us further afield, to London perhaps, who knew?

"In the words of our Prime Minister, you've never had it so good."

We had entered a world of prefects, house public-speaking competitions, cricket in summer, rugby in winter and always, it seemed, the conjugation of Latin verbs: amo, amas, amat.

I did see Lucy again though. The scandal of whatever took place at the Dingle never extended beyond the hushed tones of shock, never reached the local press, nor did it result in her drowning. I was cycling home from school and she was heading up to the High Street pushing a pram. It had been just over a year but she looked a lot older, her hair darker than I remembered and from that distance there was no sign of that gleam in her face. She did have the distinctive gap in her teeth though, it could only be Lucy. Lucy who had once told me down at the Dingle that I was useless at getting down from trees but that I was alright.

My bike still had the paintwork and chrome shine of an eleven-plus success present, my satchel was stuffed with heavy text books but above all, the yellow braid around my blazer said, loud and clear, this is who I am now. Neither of us would be going back to the Dingle but the Honey Slow River, in spate or as a summer dribble, would continue to course through both of us. I smiled and took one hand from the handlebars in greeting,

"Lucy!"

Intent on her path and leaning her weight against the gradient, Lucy Loosemore looked up, looked right at, and then straight through me.

The Whole of the Moon

It was the shouting which dragged me from fitful sleep to wakefulness. Urgent, tormented shouting in the early hours of the morning. From somewhere within or outdoors? In the murk of regaining full consciousness, it was difficult to tell.

A moment's quiet and then it came again, more pain and more anguish, from somewhere outside surely. I didn't know the time but I knew that daylight hadn't yet crept around our corner. Shouting and shouting in a language I didn't understand.

There are often incidents in that street, usually just after closing time, and being a witness is not necessarily a good thing. If you say you didn't hear anything, no-one can prove otherwise, and if you say you didn't see anything then you aren't a witness. But you can't forget.

The shouting, a wild, inarticulate howl, if some poor sod is suffering then continuing to lie in bed ignoring it doesn't sit well. It's difficult to live with inaction, difficult to square it with your conscience. With that in mind, I pulled back the duvet and swivelled on my arse to clear my legs from the bed, trying not to make too much noise, trying not to groan. I knew my way through the dark to the smaller bedroom and the window which would give me a better view of the street below, and

I padded my way across the landing like an animal ignoring the objections from aching muscles and joints. Not wanting to draw any fire to myself, I left the lights switched off. And I was right, standing by the side of the window, in what used to be my bedroom, afforded the best view of the street below. It was a good clear line of sight as the streetlights did their work but there was nothing to see. Nothing untoward at least. Most of the tiny front gardens were now being paved over to become car standing spaces. Other cars were parked haphazardly wherever possible alongside or sometimes half on and half off the pavement. Anyone trying to push a pram along there later would struggle, later when it would be busy with Saturday morning workers, shoppers, the milk delivery, papers and the post, but for now there was no visible human presence; no-one taking an early smoke, a pre-dawn stroll, or, for whatever reason, no-one yelling blue murder.

Still, there was something compelling about that view of the houses cast in the unreal glow of the neon light, and I would have stayed, witness to an inactive world, if it hadn't been for the slight noise and movement behind me. I turned and looked towards the open doorway to where the silhouetted figure of my father, dead these past two years, stood looking towards me.

"I'm sorry, I didn't mean to startle you."

"No, you're okay. It's that dressing gown, I thought you were someone else."

"It was hanging on the door," she said, "I thought I would pop it on rather than walk about in the nick. It's miles too big for me."

"It was my father's. I haven't got round to putting it away anywhere yet."

"Your father's no longer with you?"

"No, he died two years ago."

"I'm sorry."

She was standing next to me now and she leaned in to give me a hug which was peculiarly chaste after what we'd been doing some six hours earlier.

"Why are you out of bed?" she asked.

"The shouting, didn't you hear it?"

"No," she shook her head, "You were very restless though."

It was my turn to make an apology which she waved away.

"No worries. Look, it's a bit early for breakfast, but I'll make us a coffee and we'll have a chat."

I was impressed that she thought there might be enough food in the house to make some breakfast. Coffee though, we were okay for coffee as I'd just bought a new jar from Fine Fare the previous day.

"A chat? What do you want to chat about?"

"We can chat about anything, you could tell me about your dad, if you like. Or you could go on about what you were saying last night in the pub."

The pub? People at my physio group had told me that the Fox and Grapes on a Friday night was usually a good crack and so I'd said I'd maybe drop in. That's how I came to be standing there propping up a bar room wall while groups of drinkers, sitting under clouds of cigarette smoke, talked loudly, too loudly, supping pints and popping dry roasted peanuts. Of course, there was no-one there from my *come-on-push-yourself-you-can-do-it* physio group and I could reflect on how, instead of sitting at home alone drinking beer from a can, I could stand there alone drinking from a pint glass.

Some big gob kept sounding off about music. The same song kept being played over and over again, something about seeing the whole of the moon and Big Gob had said,

"Bloody rubbish! No-one's seen the whole of the moon."

Now, don't get me wrong, I didn't mind this guy sounding off at all, I could ignore him, except that I didn't like the way he was talking over people all the time, almost shouting down the women. I had some mates who would have shut him up sharpish. Johnno, Walt and Mick wouldn't have any truck with people getting above themselves like that and shouting the odds. They would have brought their fists to bear on the matter. I was learning though, this was the new me, or the me I was trying very hard to be - I used my mouth.

"Michael Collins. He stayed on board Apollo 11 orbiting the moon while Armstrong and Aldrin were practising their golf shots. Michael Collins must have seen the whole of the moon."

I hardly knew anyone in the pub, but that got a laugh and Big Gob, to his credit, conceded.

"A good point, my man, a sound counter, but my general opinion is this: pop songs are ill-equipped to say anything meaningful about the human condition.

And that was when I got it. His bald statements and bravado were not about right and wrong, fact or fiction, they were springboards for debate, for following a line of thought to see where it took you, to see if anyone could top your line. Pints were being supped and beer mats were being reflectively toyed with until the woman in the corner, the tidy brunette wearing a Born in the USA tee-shirt, took up the challenge.

"Now it's you who's talking bloody rubbish, Phil. Pop music captures a mood in an instant. It can hook into your psyche quicker than any other art form."

"Art form?" He loaded a ton of ridicule into two short words.

"Sure," she was quick to counter, "*I'm walkin' on sunshine and don't it feel good?* There you go, tap into that."

I liked the girl's spirit and the exchange was being enjoyed by the other drinkers who looked towards Phil for his response.

"Walking on sunshine? Vacuous nonsense. It's no more possible to walk on sunshine than it is to see the dark side of the moon."

"Of course it's not possible. Pop lyrics go well beyond the literal." She was fired now. "Take Bruce, for instance," she pointed to the tee-shirt image across her chest, "He's on fire."

"Bruce Springsteen? Someone *should* set him on fire."

Another laugh for Phil, so it was time to step in again.

"She's right. It's all made up, it's all glorious metaphor pointing out emotional truths."

"Yeah!"

I'd picked up some support and suggestions were being thrown out to back up my on the hoof theory and the shouted discussion continued.

"Everybody wants to rule the world."

"That's not metaphor, that's just generalisation."

"Like a virgin touched for the very first time."

"Madonna? Like a virgin? Now that does call for a lot of imagination."

More laughter, shared now, nobody targeted and I realised that if Johnno, Walt and Mick had been there,

57

it would have been a session of piss-taking, sinking a lot more beer and then handing out a good thumping to someone. But my thoughts were interrupted by the tee-shirt wearing Bruce Springsteen fan now standing right in front of me.

"Hi, I'm Sue and I want to buy a beer for the man who knows about emotional truth."

"Well Sue, you make a good coffee, I'll give you that."

We'd transferred to the kitchen and we sat around the wobbly table nursing our mugs. If she was unimpressed by the lop-sided units and the general air of squalor, she wasn't letting on. It turns out that chatting really was her thing. She'd asked about Dad and seemed to be interested in my response.

"Taciturn, wasn't he? Cumbrian through and through. He would always weigh up all the evidence before reaching a conclusion. A man of the Left. Believed implicitly in the dignity of the working man. God knows what he would have made of all this unemployment. As for that harridan..."

Sue laughed. "Not one of his favourites?"

"No, certainly not. Mind you, I don't think he cared much for Kinnock either. A windbag, he called him."

Another laugh. "A difficult man to please then?"

"Well, no, not really. Treat people with respect and be honest in your dealings and Dad would approve. Hugh Gaitskell was his man. Best Prime Minister we never had, he always said."

"I like the sound of your dad; I think I would have liked him."

"You sure? I don't think he was a big fan of Bruce Springsteen."

She took that in good part, even offering me another coffee and after she plonked the mug down in front of me, I asked her about herself, who was she when she wasn't buying beer for strange men in pubs.

"After I graduated, I thought that was it. I'd proved a point, no need for any further ambition. I could settle down and become a good Marks and Spencer wife."

"And?"

"It was Mr Wonderful, wasn't it? He didn't make a long-term payment on marital bliss and before long his eye was wandering. I'll give him his due though, he wasn't prepared to pretend any more than I was, so we split."

"And now what?"

"Now, in a superb piece of irony, I'm a Sales Supervisor for Marks and Spencer and I go home to spend the evenings with a glass of wine, Dale Spender and Andrea Dworkin."

She looked at me half-expectantly, and I paused, not wanting to fluff this open goal.

"Feminist writers, yes?"

"Yes," she said smiling and wisely not pressing me any further. Instead, she decided to probe.

"And what about you Adam? I'll give you three minutes on the last five years of your life."

It's not a conversation topic I relish. There's no point in avoiding it though so I usually say something about serving Her Majesty and making sure I kept my head well down. But I sensed that I would need a much better brand of washing powder for Sue, so I was quite up front about it, about what was the most significant ten weeks of my life.

"I was in the Falklands."

With the brainless and the Gung-Ho, that usually prompts a clamour for glorification or titillating detail. Not Sue, she just held on to her mug, maintained eye-contact and invited further disclosure.

"I did what I was trained to do, I lost some mates and now I sit at home nursing my own medical discharge."

Now she did speak, dropping her voice as though there was someone else in the house we could possibly disturb.

"Adam, you don't have to talk about this if you don't want to."

But I think she knew as well as I did, that I was about to spill my insides.

"When I say I lost some mates, that wasn't down in the South Atlantic, it was when we got back. I lost them to booze, gambling, fighting and other stuff as well, anything that takes you anywhere else. We don't meet up. If we did, we would just try and recreate something that wasn't there and it would just send us further down the road to mental. I wind them up."

"Adam, you're being hard on yourself." She put down her mug and reached across and held my hand. "You said it yourself; you did what you were trained to do."

"Exactly. What we were trained to do. You can't educate a man to kill another man, but you can train him."

Realisation spread across her features, the features I'd fancied so much in the pub: the dark eyes, the pretty upturned nose and the mouth that was made for kissing. The enormity of what I was saying registered, she needed confirmation but her words came slowly.

"Did you kill a man?"

Now it was my turn to be quiet and I neither shook nor nodded my head.

Grumbling, we all liked a good grumble, and if a chance came up to grumble about the air force or the navy boys, then all the better. April and May in the Falklands is bitter, it's their winter setting in and we'd disembarked at San Carlos to face a thirteen-mile march with full kit. The helicopter transport didn't turn up so we had to slog over sodden ground, outcrops of rock and no cover. But there was always wind, rain and fucking sleet. Language, sorry.

"You were yomping?"

"Yeah, that's what it was called."

"You were a Para?"

I looked at her closely then. I'd scored a goal by spotting her feminist writers. Was this her equaliser?"

"No, a Marine."

"And the Marines were grumbling?"

You use it don't you? Whatever gets thrown up at you, you manage it and put it to good use. Grumble as much as you like, but let it help you cover the miles; it also helps you avoid introspection. Look out for any guys who have gone too quiet. That's when the shadowy figures have broken the perimeter fence and they are racing across the compound. It's all in the head, all in the head. Warfare is ninety percent boredom – so manage it. When you see action, you'll be on that knife-edge between fight or flight. Your body will respond with either shock or an adrenalin rush, so recognise it for what it is and exercise control. It's a thin line between hero and coward.

That's how we were trained and I had some more to grumble about. I'd missed my footing on a grassy outcrop, twisted my ankle and crashed to the ground. With an eighty-pound pack on your back anyone would struggle to stay upright but I got to my feet and realised straight away the extent of my problem. I was in bloody agony and struggling to keep up. I couldn't drop out though, there would be no valour in reporting to the medical boys. We'd been ordered to wipe up any pockets of resistance and score an easy victory at Goose Green.

Of course, you never fully trust the intelligence you've been given. The Argentinians, and I always call them that, the Argentinians were much stronger than we expected and much better dug in. There wasn't a lot of natural cover, no trees, but it was rolling terrain and they'd used the natural contours well. We kept stumbling over their defensive positions and scattering as their bullets flew in our direction.

And that's how it happened, I think, if I say now, it was all a blur it sounds naff, but in amongst the gunfire, mortar explosions and shouting, I got detached. My ankle was giving me hell but I was trying to channel my adrenaline, re-join my group and charge into action. I have to admit though that I wasn't the highly-trained Marine doing his duty, it was probably more of a rampage, flailing about in amongst the darkness and the shouting looking for my course to be re-plotted. The nearest shouting was coming from somewhere just ahead of me; incoherent howling, but still, I felt it was where I should be. I set off on another charge, lurched over a hillock and came face to face with the uniformed figure lying with his back raised against a slight slope.

His was the incoherent shouting: a torrent of panic-struck Spanish.

María, Madre de Dios sálvame!

What the hell was he shouting? I'd no idea, but when he stopped waving his rifle about in a random fashion and began to train it on me, that's when the Marine asserted himself. That's when I did what I was trained to do.

Sue strengthened her grip on my hand and she probably has no idea how much comfort was gleaned from that small act. Four years on and that was the first civvy to whom I had told that story in full. The slough being shed.

"And that's the best I can do in answering your question." I told her.

"You killed a man." It was a statement not a question and my clarification stuck in my throat.

"No… no… I didn't…" She had pushed me to this moment, to the point of saying the words out loud for the first time. "Not a man. I killed a kid. I doubt if he was even eighteen years old. A conscript almost certainly and while he was flailing his rifle and shouting, possibly for his mother, I shot him at close range."

I couldn't look at her, I couldn't face whatever expression she held. I folded my arms across the table and put down my head. I wanted to cry but couldn't. Nor could I make any move. What would happen from here I had no idea. She could discreetly gather her stuff together and leave and there was nothing I could do about it; my body was solid and immobile and yet tearing apart.

How long we spent there I don't know. She didn't leave, she pulled a chair up close, laid an arm across my shoulders and put her head down onto the back of mine. Eventually, when she did speak, her voice was lowered to a soothing whisper.

"Adam, we've got time, we've got all the time we could possibly need. What you've done, facing up to the truth like that, is one of the bravest things I've ever seen or heard."

I had to look at her now. I wasn't interested in validations of actions, of estimations of bravery, it was the thing about time she had said. *All the time we could possibly need.* I must have been wearing incomprehension across my face causing her to smile.

"Next week, I thought I'd bring some bacon along and some bread rolls for some sarnies."

"Next week?"

"Next Friday. We don't need to go to the pub. We could do something else." My lack of response must have stalled her because she added, "A little bit presumptuous?"

"No," I said, and *I* wanted to smile now. It was one of those times to recognise what's happening and respond. Take control, don't look around for someone or something else to blame but time to seize the moment. Sue, the Bruce Springsteen fan, had been in and had a look around. She'd met the wounded hero and she probably knew enough to call out his bullshit. The hero was a mess and so was the house in which he rattled around. She must know about his demons, the shouting in the nights and all that, yet she was talking about plans for the following weekend, about making a decent breakfast. It was time to respond. "I was thinking I should get some decent coffee in and give that percolator a good clean." I lobbed the idea back and let it settle. "Also, a little presumptuous?"

"No," she said, "That sounds about right. We can take it from there."

The Charity of Women

Stand on the crag and look across the water to the valley mouth. Look towards the Jaws of Borrowdale, the jaws which may be an opening to heavenly pleasures on earth or an entrance to Hell itself. Brace yourself against the might of Skiddaw, imperious in the fading afternoon light, and the surrounding peaks of Blencathra, Grisedale and Causey Pike. Breathe the air and register the sights which can make the soul thrill and the heart despair. The Northern fells and lakes; for good or ill, this is the place which always calls me back.

I am with my father, renting a cottage for a week, and he never tires of telling the tale of how, as a lad, he was sent from the industrial coast to spend a summer in this Cumbrian village. We spent a morning trailing round narrow streets asking could this be the place? Could this be it? Trying to locate the cottage where he was assigned by his adult carer to scan the outline of the fells for the return of the walkers, to give warning of their impending return and of the necessity for the kettle to be boiled and the teapot filled for massing.

"You were sent away from home? How old were you then?"

"No more than eight. I started school at eight and left at eleven." I mull over this piece of information and he continues. "She was very kind was Mrs Graham, giving me daily tasks: make my bed, sweep out and wash dishes. She only ever raised her voice once, when she caught me hefting the coal bucket into the cottage from the back yard."

Additions to the well-worn story and I wonder why lifting a coal bucket should be such an offence.

"My chest. I had to protect my chest." And I have no need to question further as I know about the T.B. which had shadowed his young years and tailed him into adulthood. "Otherwise, once I had completed my tasks, I was free to run wild."

He gestures towards the expanse of landscape where a mist was beginning to rise over the fields and I nod in appreciation.

"You were lucky."

"I was. There was Mrs Graham and three other women who were very good to me in my lifetime: my mother, my grandmother and my wife – your mother that is - and now…now I never see any of them."

"No, of course not."

I place my hand over his as though this rare expression of emotion demands a physical response and I am making a small breach in the wall of reserve which has always kept us apart. I do not question how he had ranked those three women, nor do I pick up on the mere three years of education he'd had, knowing that it would touch a nerve. I've heard him say many a time, "Held me back, did that, held me back my whole life, that lack of schoolin'."

It would do to sit for a while and reflect, to watch a late summer evening gracefully give way to nightfall and to think over the day's events: the joy of quartering the lake on the public launch, and then the return, into a headwind and water choppier than earlier, in our seats deep in the bow, experiencing first-hand, the dipping of the prow towards the black depths and the rising above the white tops. We grimaced in the face of spitting spray, and my father, the man who had urged toughness on the sports field, the man who had shown little sympathy for any of my boyhood trepidations, holding onto the rubber-covered bar in front of us, his knuckles shining white in his fierce grip as we faced the rising and plunging, and something I had never seen before: his face clouded with apprehension. I felt an urge to put an arm around him which I rejected, still not man enough to acknowledge frailty and fear. We would continue to face our peaks and troughs as separate bodies.

When we finally reached the main jetty, we clambered unsteadily up the wooden steps and then picked our way carefully across the rocks and pebbles at the lake's edge. I had wanted to find a tea shop, having long since learned that tea was a universal comfort after any trauma no matter how minor, and the urge to win approval never waned. But he demurred.

"I need the toilet."

"We'll find one at the café."

"No, I want to go back to our cottage."

We'd touched upon expressing emotion that afternoon and now we'd encountered the embarrassment of the need for a toilet, the prospect of an accident and the dread of what such an event would cause. The changing roles of father and son had always been a line over which we would never step; the child becomes the father and the cared for becomes the carer. A future of sans teeth, sans taste did not bear thinking about, let alone discussing. We were much more comfortable sitting on this bench outside our cottage watching the evening glow.

Two buzzards, our distant companions throughout our stay, wheel high in the sky and draw attention with their high-pitched scream.

"You warm enough, Dad? Do you need a thicker jumper?"

He emits a grumble and I think it is because I am over-fussing, but fetching a jumper is something I can do, although it would be further ingratiation, but it is not this which causes his irritation, it is the figure of Bill loping up the path towards us. He will sit down without invitation and begin grumbles of his own after our greeting.

"It's been a grand day, Bill."

He makes no immediate response and I am left to think about my use of the word, *grand*, a word I would not usually use, altering my diction to find favour. The eager pup will not lie down although none of this appears to register with Bill.

"Been into town today. Place is full of bloody tourists."

It's the inward worm which gnaws at Bill, he who has gained more than most from the industry plaguing his beloved Vales. His, is still the best-selling guidebook to the Lakes. And weren't we, my father and I, weren't we also bloody tourists? Dad might have sensed some of this, he might object in private to Bill's constant complaints and his dark frowning, but he always suffers his presence. Company is always company, even if the direction of talk is uncomfortable. Besides, Dad can hold his own, he is perfectly capable of jabbing and moving or landing the conversational knock-out blow if need be. But there is something which draws these two together, something to which I am not party, and maybe I would be best advised to watch and learn. Poet and adult role model; these are the two men I have always admired. Dad's tolerance of Bill is something I can usefully develop instead of my readiness to snap at inconsistencies.

"Come on, Bill, you've said yourself that your work should speak the language of the common man. You can't complain if the common man then turns up in a flock to see what it is that you've been extolling."

"Turning up is one thing, being open to what you find is another."

I know this man to be solemn, taciturn and sometimes downright rude. Now though, he looks ready to launch into one of his sermons and I seek to head him off. "Don't give me that learning from Nature stuff, that Nature as a moral guide twaddle. We learn our morality from other people, from respecting people, not from deriding them for being populous."

I'm not sure if that is the right word or not. I'd said populous but I was trying to get at his elitist condescension, and I think he may have caught my meaning.

"Nature is constant whereas people often make poor teachers. From some there is nothing to learn, but take your father, who is a good man, he's told me about the summer he spent here as a boy. That summer up here surrounded by the fells and all the glory will have shaped his character more than anything else."

And now another word springs to mind – hypocrite. I don't wait to see if my father agrees, he will speak up if he wants to, me though, I am going to take Bill to task.

"That's a bit rich. Aren't you the one who wrote about London. The one who sang the praises of London, London with all its smoke, slums and destitution, and you, you said that earth had nothing more beautiful than the view from that bloody bridge across the river."

Again, patience is something I could usefully learn, patience or at least a little restraint. Respect for your elders, an old-fashioned value perhaps, but it wouldn't hurt to let Bill have his little grumble. He is getting on. I should be offering to make him a cup of tea, not railing against what he'd spoken and written years ago. So, his values have changed, his flame has long since dimmed, it happens, and he is unlikely to be coming back at me. At least, that's what I'm thinking.

"You know nothing." Bill does have a response. "I found out an early age what we can learn from people. Oh yes, I learned of the kindness of women, their charity. I knew the love of my mother who died when I was eight years old. The despair of being parted from my dear sister and the joy in our hearts when we were re-united and our insistence that we would never again be parted. And that day you speak of, the day we left by coach from London, crossing Westminster Bridge as we set off for France bound to meet up with the woman I loved and the daughter I barely knew, that day I wrote of what was in my heart."

His implication is clear. What *do* I know? What life experience can I offer up against his and how dare I challenge his view? The buzzards, barely visible now, scream again. He is not passionate, or angry, he is speaking in measured terms.

"But I also know full well what we can learn from men. I have seen carts carrying their prisoners to a dreadful fate. Gorsas and the Girondin, and I've seen the look in their eyes, not fear and not hate, but, for their fellow men gathered in their hordes for a blood-soaked vision of justice, just sheer contempt. Before the guillotine that was, before the guillotine's blade." He pauses and I did dare not speak; let him continue. "Don't talk to me about liberty or fraternity. If I have come to put my faith in Nature, then I have just cause."

The pause now extends my father's silence, but then eventually he looks towards me and breaks his peace. "That girl, the one *you* knew at college, do you ever think of her?"

The girl at college? I play for some time, startled by my father speaking of affairs of the heart. Startled too by the way that dying embers can spark and flare. But I do not need to consider for too long.

"From time to time, Yes, she showed some kindness towards me."

A weak deflection of the question.

"Did you treat her badly?"

There is a lot to be said for silence, for gazing at the world and taking stock. The last rays of the sun have died beyond Skiddaw. There is no more screaming from the buzzards, it is the jackdaws now breaching the peace, croaking their mockery. Bill fades into the dying light to be mocked in his absence, the eighteenth century radical now scorned for lauding flowers by a lakeside, but he would always be the firebrand that I would never be. The girl at college? She'd seen through my poetic bombast and packed her bags. My father too, now takes his leave, slipping his hand out from under mine and going back to wherever.

I nurse my loss and I mourn again, for the woman whose charity I'd spurned, and for my father, who must have felt his disappointment keenly.

They are rare now, my father's visits.

How the Northern Light Gets In

One

Among the secret whispers of dark night, animal rustlings and the wind blowing over the rough grass he heard those words over and over again, *just hope I'm here when you come back.*

Otherwise, her silence had been loud, almost as loud as her deeds. She had stormed around completing housework tasks with heavy emphasis and he knew it was best to withdraw. She'll come round he thought. She always does…eventually.

For his part he could pack his rucksack with the relish he had for his kit. Everything lightweight, everything designed to keep out the cold, wind and rain. His kit made him invincible.

"I could do without this you know." She broke her vow of angry silence. "We've got people coming and you think this is a good time to go gallivanting on the fells."

"People?"

"This is no time for being funny. My parents are coming as you damn well know and you decide to take off for an overnighter."

Ah, yes, Bill and Wendy of the publicly displayed liberal disposition and the privately conveyed heavy insinuation. Was their daughter's partner aware of the benefits of getting on to the property ladder? That it was never too early to think about a pension? And if there was to be something permanent in his partner status, then their stockpiled weapon of choice was the heavy hint about needing more space in the future, about an extra bedroom and some play space. He seethed at their aspersions, their obsession with space when their claustrophobic presence sucked the very life out of him.

He told himself that it was just unfortunate timing that's all. Becky knew that his overnighter on Blencathra was important. Did he have to explain again? She was stiff with resentment as he made a move towards her, "I'll be back well before Bill and Wendy arrive."

"*They* think you're bloody mental. *I* think you're bloody mental. What are you expecting to see up there anyway?"

Bloody mental or not, he was well-prepared for a night abroad where wilder spirits roamed. He had checked the weather forecast; he knew the times of sunset and sunrise and he also knew that great photographs don't just land in your lap; you have to go and look for them. Becky knew that. Becky understood that.

"Go then, and just hope I'm here when you come back."

Sometimes, his one-man tent, even on the bleakest of fell-sides, had somnambulant powers. But sleep was not always a given. His thoughts churned. Timing was everything – to be there when light balanced on a fulcrum against darkness. And the words: *just hope I'm here when you come back.*

He was preoccupied until that moment when the northern fells began to reveal their outline presence, when nature turned in her circle and threw the night sky into retreat. The light was perfect and the sky defied description. For he was not a man of words; let his camera capture the moment and he pressed, pressed and pressed again the shutter on the fragile and the beautiful. He would frame his love.

"You just don't get it, do you?" Becky again; she who had once been a life force, a writer who loved words, who agonised about sentences and paid attention to the world. "I'm moving on. I'm not stuck here like one of your lumps of rock, your Hell-bloody-cathra."

"Helvellyn."

"Right, Mr High and Mighty, your Hel-bloody-vellyn. I'm moving on."

Feisty, but she had been shaken and bruised when he first met her slumped on a pavement as a street protest began to turn violent.

"Let's get out of here," he'd said, "Too many people."

That's how I picked her up he always used to joke, until she told him that that wasn't funny, but he'd known immediately. As soon as he'd seen the dark hair falling across her forehead and the eyes which blazed with passion, he had known. This was a girl he could take back to Cumbria where he would show her how the northern light gets in. Now though, her flame was dwindling, she was still responding to the pluck of mum and dad, still twitching at their pursed lips and oblique comments; they who had always dreamed of a gilt-framed photograph to stand on their Lakeland slate hearth. Had Becky lost sight of the dream or had it always been his dream alone, his celebration of northern fells and wild northern skies?

That she was pulling on a separate rein, finally became evident one night under the duvet. The question was carelessly posed but it had opened up parts of a picture he hadn't seen, but he'd answered it through his very presence and deeds. Or at least he thought he had. Why reduce such wonder to the limitation of words? He'd said *yes* for a quiet life. He didn't want the earnest discussion which could escalate into a row, or worse still, the silence. He'd also said yes because he meant it.

Now he stood on a ridge of a mighty fell, an insignificant figure before the morning light which flooded in from the east while the night time constellations faded at his back. No, he was not a man of words but he knew he had to think. And no, he didn't get it. They had what they had always wanted. There was more? He thought about their terraced house with Bill and Wendy picking out comments as though they were removing slugs from a salad. Rented or not though, it was *their* terraced house, his and Becky's. He thought about it again, how snug it could be with the open fire blazing and coffee mugs cupped between warm hands. And then, how it might be, empty, echoing only the busy sounds of the family next door. The busy sounds of the *family* next door.

Looking to the distance he could see the Vale of St John's and to the east the Helvellyn range emerging from the grey mist. The sun was picking out scattered whitewashed farmhouses and below him a kestrel hovered on the still point. This mighty land was stretching into the morning. *Here is my space*, he told himself before finally picking up his rucksack.

He'd reviewed the shots he'd taken but he'd need to look at them in more detail later, now it was time to make a move. *Sod them, sod them both.* This wasn't about being compliant with the pressure of in-laws, this was something he and Becky would do; the two of them, him and Becky and…whoever. He'd said *yes* and he had meant yes. The light had entered the darkness, his camera hung round his neck, the rucksack sat comfortably on his shoulders and it was time to make a move. So, invincible and crushed, fired and diminished, he knew, it was time, and Becky would like this…not sure whether it was a metaphor or an analogy, anyway, he knew now that it was time for him to come down from the mountain.

But the serious photographer should never switch off and he should always have his camera to hand.

Two

The vixen had been a proper fox, not an urban scrounger but a rural, demonised, mythologised fox leading her cubs towards food, and the morning light had picked out the party in striking silhouette. Serendipity had been his friend; he had the shots to download and process. This wouldn't be his terrified Vietnamese girl screaming with napalm burns, nor a striking miner in a copper's helmet, but it might be his long shot of the passenger jetty reaching out over the lake. The Cumbrian fells, the animal of local lore and an appeal to public sentiment; the artist in him couldn't withstand his commercial speculation.

His was a confident stride. Becky though, how was she feeling? Had the storm within her abated overnight? Had her threats lost their charge? Would she even be there in the house when he got back? They needed to sit down and talk, and goodness knows, he had a lot to offload. Because what had become clear to him during the long night alone amongst the elements, what became clear to him whenever he spent such a night away, was that Becky and he had something, something which they shouldn't allow to be lost just because life was moving on. Being students had been fun, moving in together had been an adventure, what lay ahead of them should be a joy and he would tell her that.

It was still early, those whose business demanded it were already up and about, but for the most part the morning was still stretching, flexing a few muscles for more concentrated action later, but as he rounded the corner, the sight hit him like a thump to the chest. The flashing blue light of a stationary ambulance outside their house. He checked the impulse to run, but hurried along the pavement anyway, hardening himself against whatever was to come, blocking off the avenues of worst-case scenario, but Becky, Becky!

Becky who, as if by telepathic connection, opened the front door and met him stony-faced.

"It's Donna. She's in trouble. They're taking her to Carlisle."

"The baby?"

"The baby is still okay, as far as we know."

Others were beginning to emerge from their houses to stand in whispering groups. Casual walkers stopped in sympathy, curious and helpless. Most of them knew of the young woman at number 12 who already had one kid with another on the way.

"I'm going with her." Becky was resolute. "In the ambulance, I'm going with her."

"To Carlisle?"

"Yes, to Carlisle, Newcastle, Timbuktu, wherever."

"I thought she had a partner for all this." Matt was dredging his memory of what he had been told about Next Door's arrangements.

"She does, but she can't get here at this notice. You'll be in charge."

The morning he'd envisaged evaporated.

"In charge?"

"Yes, young Nicky. Get him some breakfast, reassure him, keep him occupied, put the tv on if you have to."

Matt was aware of the boy who was standing not two metres away from them, white-faced, unkempt, and uncomprehending. Matt wasn't sure how old the boy was, nor how he would keep him occupied. He was at a loss, taken aback by these events, the suddenness of it all, his own inadequacy.

"Becky...?"

Bystanders shuffled aside as Donna was wheeled out towards the gaping doors of the ambulance.

"Becky...?"

But there was no time now, nor did she moderate her tone in front of the young boy.

"Look, Matt, whatever you do, don't fuck this up."

Three

With officers in pairs standing on corners and in shop doorways and their vans parked up side streets, most of the town centre Saturday shoppers had noticed the increased police activity and had taken the cue to complete their errands and find their way home. The young officers were smiling and chatting together, eager even to engage with passers-by, and always trying to look relaxed but the atmosphere was tense. Summat was up.

Matt knew about the projected rally and that was why he was there with his camera; it was just a question of anticipating any opportunities and finding the best position to catch them. Whether to opt for a vantage point and stick, or follow the march as it progressed.

"You've got a lot of people out. You expecting trouble?"

One of the officers turned to Matt and made a quick appraisal before answering.

"No, expecting to prevent trouble. You media?"

No. Freelance, me. Came along just in case."

"Well, you might be disappointed. All gob and no back-up this lot."

"Pro-Britain?"

"That's them. They're starting in the Albion, heading up this way and then round to the town hall."

Matt looked at the young police officer and his equally young colleague who would be expected to be first in action in the case of violence breaking out.

He tried to take a discreet look at the weaponry they had around their bodies, wondering whether they were all issued with sticks and tasers and whether there could ever be enough training to equip a person to enter a physical encounter and exercise judicious use of force.

"No, I hope I am disappointed. I hope you all have a quiet afternoon."

"Thanks, mate. The Town Hall might be your best bet though. That's where the other lot will be."

"The other lot?"

"The Freedom from Fascism lot: students, hippies and the great unwashed."

Matt smiled and then immediately wondered whether his reaction constituted agreement, support, or some kind of mealy-mouthed compliance.

"Right, I'll have a walk up there then."

However, he turned back down towards the Albion pub.

He slipped his camera inside his coat before he entered the pub where his arrival attracted some attention. More appraisal; if he was not a regular, the next step was to establish if he was a sympathiser.

"Are you here for the march?"

Matt looked at the young man who had spoken to him.

"Are you in charge?"

"Not really, I've got the details of the route, I've got leaflets to hand out and at twelve o'clock, I'll get everyone on the move."

"So, you are in charge."

"Again, no." The man smiled, "I'm a mere functionary."

Matt took a more serious interest in the smiling man before him; the man who was dressed more smartly than the other customers in the pub, the man who used words like *functionary*. Having just met him, it would be bad form to offer to buy him a drink, and anyway, he was a bit pushed for cash.

"Okay, a functionary might be able to give me some more information. Let me get a drink and we'll talk some more, if you've got the time."

"Sure."

"Can I get you one?"

"No thanks, I'll keep a clear head for this."

The Albion was a new pub for Matt. He took in the general air of grubbiness: walls which needed repainting and carpets replaced; the tables were chipped and stained, but set against that, Matt was served with an impressive looking pint. He preferred golden bitters to dark stouts and this one had a creamy head of foam overlapping the rim of the glass. He took his first mouthful and then returned to the man with the leaflets and the plan.

"Okay, so what's this all about?"

"Good question and I can give you a good answer. Things have come to a head. There's a whole section of the British workforce which has been ignored. Look around you at the lads in this pub; they should all have good jobs in industry, in steel and coal, good honest physical jobs. But those jobs have all gone. There's nowt there now."

Matt noted the rising passion in the voice and the return of an accent which had been hitherto been concealed.

"Well, that's not exactly true, is it?"

"Why? What else is there? You wanna work in a call-centre, or a warehouse? What is it you do anyway?"

Matt took the opportunity to take another pull from his pint and consider his options. He was a student; he also took photographs and he didn't think that either answer would court any favour.

"I'm a student."

"Student, eh? Well, I'm wondering what you're doing down here. Shouldn't you be up the hill with the other layabouts?"

"Layabouts? Are we stereotyping now?"

"No," the man laughed and held up his hand. "No, I'm not stereotyping, I'm just making a bitter comment about education and how its privileges are strictly rationed, out of reach of the people I've just been talking about. Not only have they taken our jobs but they've given us crap schools as well. There's no way out."

"No way out of…?"

"This. Rubbish schools, rubbish housing, rubbish services and no future. That's why we're here today; the British working classes are making a stand and getting their voices heard."

"So, you want British jobs for British people. Free speech for the British and no foreigners – kick 'em out. On with the Union Jack tee-shirts."

"Now who's stereotyping?"

Matt picked up his pint again and then paused before lifting it to his mouth.

"I'm sorry. Lazy thinking."

"Apology accepted. I'm Pete, Pete Lawson." He held out his hand to shake now. "What're you gonna do with the camera?"

Matt was unaware that the camera was showing and he sheepishly covered it.

"I do a bit of freelancing. I thought I might take a few shots today."

"Fine. Well, march with us. Take your shots from our side. T.V. or Press, we always get shown as the aggressors. Let people see what we face."

The pub had filled and most of the seats were taken. The noise level too had risen with several groups of men standing around talking and shouting over each other. From somewhere within the building tension a guffaw suddenly erupted followed by a shout:

"No Surrender!"

And a chorused response:

"One World Cup and two World Wars!

And more laughter which rolled in an echo around the pub. Matt leaned across to Pete, "Are these your downtrodden and neglected English working class? Because they're acting like yobs at the moment. This won't win any sympathy votes."

Pete gave a thin smile, "Who wants sympathy votes? What you've got here are some proud lads. Don't say they haven't got a case just because they lack a bit of polish. No social justice until they show good manners? I don't think so. And anyway, did you miss the note of irony?"

It was a relief to get out of the crowded pub at the appointed time. Pete had slipped away from Matt and he now stood on a low wall marking the boundary of the pub car park speaking through a megaphone.

"Okay, these lads with the banner will take the lead. Remember, this is a march, not a stampede. Take your time, show respect to those who watch and cheer. And remember, we have our good friends here to guide us to the Town Hall."

At the mention of good friends there was a muted ironic cheer and someone shouted,

"They could give us a lift with all those vans!"

When the laughter stopped, Pete added,

"And remember lads, no bother today eh. Even if someone is looking to start something."

There was a muttered, "If someone wants to start something, we'll be ready."

Matt, less circumspect about having a camera now, checked the settings and switched it on to standby as the newly formed crocodile began to lurch its way behind the flimsy banner towards the Town Hall.

The beer-fuelled protest movement began to make its voice heard.

"England for the English!"

Four

Matt opened his eyes and adjusted to his situation which slowly emerged. His favourite armchair in the small front room of the cottage where the tv in the corner played at low volume; nearby was his rucksack which he'd dumped on his return and there, on the sofa, the young boy from next door.

"You fell asleep."

There was little point in denying the obvious. Matt looked towards the clock on the mantelpiece to try and establish just how long he had been asleep but gave up the mental calculation when he realised, he didn't know what time he had dropped off.

"It's Nicky, isn't it?"

"Yes."

"What are you watching, Nicky?"

"Dunno."

"Are you enjoying it though?"

"Dunno."

"Well, let's switch it off, shall we and we'll make a plan."

The boy didn't respond, so Matt hauled himself out of the chair, staggered sleepily across the room and switched off the tv before turning back to the boy.

"You don't say a lot, do you Nicky?"

As the picture on the screen disappeared, Nicky turned his gaze back towards Matt.

"They said you were going to look after me."

"Who did?"

"The people who took Mum away."

"Ah, yes. Well, let's sort all that out, shall we? The people who took your mum away are the ambulance people. They're going to look after your mum while she's feeling poorly. They're good people. And you know Becky who lives in this house, she's also gone with your Mum to be her friend. Becky is a good person."

"Is Becky your friend?"

"Yes, she is, but she can also be your mum's friend. Okay, everything sorted?"

"Is Becky a good person?"

"Yes, I've already said, Becky is a good person and also a beautiful person."

Becky's goodness had been established, her beauty or otherwise, did not concern Nicky. He had his own statement to make,

"My mum's going to have a baby."

Matt looked at the boy from next door and wondered why he had had so little to do with him or his mum. He also wondered what the boy had been told.

"Mum says I can have a baby brother or a baby sister."

Somehow or other, this boy had been led to believe that the gender of the baby would be a matter of his choice. Matt was beginning to understand something about the difficulties of communicating with children and how attempted simplifications could lead to further complications. Brother or sister, boy or girl, the even more difficult question of the likelihood of the baby's safe arrival was beyond Matt. He would not issue platitudes or groundless reassurances without a basis of truth. Still, he had been left in charge and he should see to that.

"Have you had any breakfast, Nicky? What do you like?"

The boy looked blank.

"For breakfast, what do you like for breakfast?"

"Dunno."

It occurred to Matt that being in charge probably meant a little more leading from the front. He would start to take direct action and if that met with Nicky's displeasure, he was sure he would soon find out.

"I'll tell you what, have you ever had eggy bread? The finest breakfast a man can have is eggy bread. It's going to be down to us though, no-one else is going to make it for us. Come on, off the sofa and we'll wash our hands before we make the breakfast of kings."

Matt quickly realised that close supervision would be needed as Nicky looked fazed by the assembly of kitchen cutlery and ingredients and he looked apprehensively at the eggs in the open carton. He had to handle them, crack them and empty them into a bowl. He'd been disturbed by the long stream of gloop hanging and dangling persistently from the broken shells. Small fragments of shell had made it into the bowl and they needed to be extracted before the sticky liquid was mixed with a fork. It was messy and awkward and it led to Nicky constantly looking up towards Matt uncertainly.

"Hey! You're doing great! Let's give it a little more oomph though. We want it well mixed."

Nicky tried a more determined approach only for some of the mixture to slop out of the bowl over the kitchen worktop. He glanced anxiously again towards

Matt who simply picked up a cloth and wiped away the mess.

Then it became even more difficult as the gas ring was lit, a drop of oil was poured into the frying pan which was placed over the ring. Flames and heat now, be careful. They used a fish slice to place the pieces of egg-soggy bread into the pan and he kept his fingers well clear as a sinister sizzling sprang from the pan in return and Matt gave him an extra instruction now to keep an eye on things.

"We don't want these to burn and we don't want a smoky kitchen. Because the Boss will be cross."

Matt was pleased with his improvised rhyme. Word plays weren't usually his thing, but Nicky gave him another anxious look.

"Becky, she's the Boss. But it's just a joke. She won't be cross."

The fish slice was brought into action again and the eggy bread was mounted on a plate and ceremoniously carried across to the kitchen table where Matt made a brief statement,

"Let us give thanks for a wonderful meal and express our gratitude for the skills of Nicky the Chef."

Nicky beamed and tried to deflect the acclaim,

"You did most of it."

"No, it was teamwork. Well done, mate! That, my friend, was a first-class effort. Give me five!"

They began to work through the pile on the plate with Nicky feeling good. When Mum came back, he would tell her about eggy bread.

Five

The beer-fuelled conviction that violence was the answer to a question which remained unclear asserted itself. Lurching towards the opposition with his mates as back-up, the man with closely cropped hair barged into a crowd of voluble antagonists and threw a series of wild punches. A flashpoint: the possibility of which had always been present but predicting the precise time and place had been difficult. Two opposing groups suddenly in close proximity and the mood changed from rowdy, boisterous posturing to malign intent in an instant. Any irony in the shouted chants was replaced by overt antagonism.

"Never surrender!"

Matt recognised a group from the pub. Without badges or slogans on their shirts, they didn't show any favours but they were intent now on inflicting maximum damage through degenerating the pushing and shoving into a fracas of swinging indiscriminate haymakers. Matt raised his camera and trained it on a red-faced man in a black sweatshirt and in doing so, he made himself a target.

"Oi!"

Matt tried to avoid the assault, ducking away from a badly aimed blow but taking the force of it on his shoulder. It was enough to send him sprawling up against a barrier and for his reactions to freeze. Fight or flight? He did neither, he was lumped in an ungainly heap, a sitting target for the next thump or kick, but the flurry of violence passed on and the only reaction he could muster was to try and ensure that his camera was safe, and to resist the reflex to vomit.

Completely unmanned, he knew that he would have to get back to his feet. He was also annoyed that he had completely misread the whole situation, being in the wrong position and missing the big shots. He climbed awkwardly over a barrier onto the pavement and edged into the crowd trying to ignore the inner suggestion that rose yet again that photo-journalism was not for him.

He still might be able to salvage something if he edged into the crowd, pushing into this group of people who were screaming and shouting rather than involving themselves in any physical violence, he might just get a telling shot. Faces, concentrate on faces, on attitudes emerging through grimaces and scowls: swagger, pride and arrogance. What he didn't see until it was almost too late was the traffic cone which came cartwheeling through the air towards him. Instinct ruled and he ducked his head to one side at the very last second. Not so lucky was the group of women protestors behind him, one of whom took a glancing blow across the temple and screamed out as she was dumped onto the pavement. When Matt turned around, she was already holding her head and squirming about on the pavement to ease the pain.

"Hey," He crouched down beside her. "How you doin'?"

"How do you think I'm doing? What the hell was that?"

"Traffic cone. Could have been worse, could have been a house brick."

"Thanks."

"Here, let me have a look." He eased her hand away from her temple. "Hmm…"

"Well…?" She looked at him for confirmation about what he could see and she could only feel.

"Some grazing, no actual broken skin. There's a lump forming and you'll probably have a massive headache tomorrow."

"It hurts like hell. Are you a doctor?"

"No, I'm a cameraman. Freelance. That cone missed me by a whisker."

"Well, you're full of consolation."

"Sorry. Do you think you can stand? Let's get out of here. Too many people."

The St John Ambulance post was already busy but they were able to provide a chair, an antiseptic wipe and a cold compress for her temple.

"If I'm tending to one of the sick and wounded, I ought to know her name at least."

"Becky. Becky Robinson. And you?"

"Matt. Matt Armstrong."

"Well, Matt Armstrong. It looks like you're my saviour. I'm going to pull through this. What were you doing? Am I keeping you from your camera work?"

"Why? What are you going to do?"

"Me? I'm going to go back and hurl some more abuse at those pillocks."

"The Pro-Britain people?"

"People? To be called people you have to able to muster at least a handful of brain cells. That lot just get a kick out of making a bloody nuisance of themselves. Show offs and bigots. They're all males, have you noticed that? Full of male entitlement, not giving a damn about anyone else."

He'd stopped his dabbing at her head with the antiseptic wipe but he wanted to start again, just so that he could hold that lovely dark hair away from her face and look at the passion which blazed from her dark blue, almost to the point of being purple, eyes. It didn't do to stare he should concentrate on what she was saying. She thought those marchers were show offs and bigots. He'd thought they were more dangerous than that. Their bluster hadn't only been bluster, they'd showed themselves to be capable of senseless, dangerous violence against which he had been unable to muster any kind of response. A few minutes ago, he'd been physically inert, completely unable to make a creditable response. If heroism was grace under pressure, he'd only demonstrated crippling fear. Now this girl, to whom he was trying to offer comfort, was all for putting herself back into the line of danger.

"It's how they get their kicks. They're not in it for anything else but an adrenaline charge. Let's give someone a good kicking."

Matt pulled back a little as if to inspect any good he'd been doing with the wipe, but really, he was trying to take in the full picture, trying to take in the image of the injured woman who only a few minutes ago had been sprawled on the pavement and he was trying to match that to the firebrand before him now spouting opposition towards the marching yobs. Only moments ago, he had been all too aware of the sick feeling of fright which had surged through his body, the irrational sense of losing his manliness because he was ill-equipped to wade in and trade punches or whatever. And here she was determined to rejoin the cause.

"Don't."

"Don't what?"

"Don't go back there for more confrontation. You've done your bit."

"And what do you suggest I do instead? Take a walk in the park? Find an armchair? Do some knitting?"

He would not back down in the face of her scorn, but he knew he needed to be a little more persuasive.

"You still need to be checked out. They'll do a concussion check and then, if you get the all-clear, they'll suggest you take it easy."

"There's nowt wrong with me. And you'll want to get back to taking your snaps." Matt smiled at the passion, the vehemence, the lurch towards vernacular language and what he hoped was her baiting. "You laughing at me?"

"No."

"What then?"

"I'm thinking how nice it would be to get that all-clear from the medics and then buy you a nice cup of tea."

"Nice! Nice! You think I can be bought out with nice? A nice cup of tea?"

"I could throw in a fruit scone as well."

Six

"What's that?"

It was the first time the pale-faced boy had shown interest in anything, the first time he had revealed any sense of curiosity.

"That's a photograph I took this morning. I like to print them off and pin them up for a while."

"What are they though?"

"Foxes. A vixen and two cubs in the early morning light. Do you like it?"

"It's alright."

"You can help me if you want. I usually stick up a little label for my pictures. Give me a title and we'll mount it. What do you think we should call it?"

The boy looked at the picture stuck to the kitchen wall.

"I dunno."

"Well, it's not that difficult. Just a title for the picture."

"Foxes."

Matt paused. What they called the picture now made absolutely no difference because he knew that its title would change before he sent it off anywhere. But still, there was scope here for a little more imagination,

"Yeah, that's good, but I think the people looking at it will know they're foxes. Is there anything else we could mention? What are they doing?"

"Looking for food."

"Yes. Spot on. So, what about, foxes looking for food? Foraging for food? Looking for breakfast?"

"Foxes looking for eggy bread."

Nicky was startled by Matt's burst of laughter.

"Oh! Nicky! That's priceless. Foxes looking for eggy bread! Brilliant! Come on, let's write the label. Grab a pen."

But Matt's surge of enthusiasm was blocked by the shutter which had suddenly closed down between himself and Nicky.

"What's the matter, Nicky?"

The boy had made no effort to reach for a pen. If anything, he was cowering away from it.

"Whoa! Nicky, are you okay? What's the problem?"

Matt had to get in close to hear the boy's muttered reply.

"I have trouble with my letters."

Matt's first instinct was to breeze past this problem and sweep it away with one extravagant statement. But the atmosphere had changed as quickly as a click of fingers, the foxes looking for eggy bread had slipped away taking the recent laughter with them. Prudence held him back, the sudden realisation that something more supportive was needed.

"Hey, I guess that makes us real partners. That was my problem at school. I was never great with letters, I wasn't a great writer, not a great reader either come to that."

Nicky raised his head to check that he hadn't been fooled earlier. Wasn't this kitchen filled with piles of books, magazines and hand-written notices pinned to the wall? He didn't need to say anything but how could this be?

"I know, I know. It got better as I got older. But do you know who really helped me?

"No."

"Becky. It was Becky who sorted me out. Do you know what she said? She said that letters, words and sentences are our friends. They want to help us, not give us problems." He waited for a flicker of acknowledgement from Nicky and then continued. "I'll tell you what we can do here. Let's talk about the titles we want to use and then I'll write them out and you can make a neat copy and we'll pin them up under each photograph. Okay? It'll look great. And when we've done that, let's go out and take some more photographs. You and me. What do you say?"

From somewhere beneath his cloak of bewildered uncertainty, Nicky managed a nod, but he still had doubts but Matt was one step ahead of him.

"Don't worry, I'll lend you a camera and I'll show you what to do. It's dead easy, okay?"

Matt knew that his Lumix Panasonic kept on automatic setting would be just the job for Nicky, and he knew that he would have to nip upstairs to pick it up. "We'll go to the lakeside for the ducks, that'll give us some great shots. Hang on."

Striding up the stairs two at a time, Matt knew he was going to enjoy the plan he had just formulated. Back to basics photography, the sort of thing he ought to be doing more often, he'd be reminding himself as much as teaching Nicky. The camera, he'd seen it just the other day, he'd pick it up and then they could be off. Stepping into the bedroom though he had to stop after his first stride and the sight that met him. Becky was a stickler for tidiness and order and making the bed was usually job number one for the day. Now, he was looking at something totally unexpected. The morning's emergency next door had clearly stopped Becky in her tracks. Here was the evidence, on top of a neatly made bed, of a job which had been started and interrupted and the work in progress left a clear message. Not that Matt could do anything about it at that moment. Much more slowly than when he had run up the stairs, he made his way around the bed to pick up the camera.

"Okay, you've got a nice steady hold on the camera and you've taken some great pictures already. Now let's see if we can get a good one of the launch, that big boat tied to the jetty."

Nicky had found that taking photographs was much easier than he'd expected. Matt had been good, giving him lots of suggestions, and when they'd looked back over the pictures he'd taken, Matt had said they were very good.

"Okay, check your viewfinder carefully, that's your screen there look, and don't just check that you've got the boat, check everything else on there as well, the jetty, that man who is helping the people to board, and then the fells right in the distance on the other side of the lake."

"Now?"

"You decide when you've got the picture you want and then press the shutter, the button on the top. You're the man with the camera, you make the decisions."

The engines on the launch suddenly coughed into life. Water surged from below the stern and the boat's departure was underway generating a swell and series of waves smacking on the lake shore. Some passengers waved at Nicky who laughed and took picture after picture as the boat motored across the water heading for the far side of the lake.

Matt looked down at Nicky and marvelled at how engaged he'd become in the photography project. He turned his own attention to the fast-receding image of the launch bound for the landing stage at Nichol End Marina on the west side of Derwentwater. That was the disembarking point for a route up the popular fell, Cat Bells. He smiled fondly at the thought of his early fell walking days and his feeling of being on top of the world at 451 metres, buffeted by the wind but with his first summit under his belt. Standing there, glorying in the panorama of the North-Western fells. Then he turned to look down the lake towards the more demanding climb of Castle Crag which stood at the mouth of the myth-laden Jaws of Borrowdale, where for him, real fell-walking had begun. It was from there he had made his first ventures up the valley towards Seathwaite, the starting point for the great climbs up the fells of central Lakeland with their imposing names: Glaramara, Broad Crag, Scafell Pike, and his especial favourite Great Gable where he had once hunkered down with Becky at the Westmorland Cairn, just below the summit, keeping as low as possible to stay out of range of the driving wind, the better to eat their cheese sandwich lunch and share the joy of triumph.

"We made it! Despite all of that grumbling, we made it!"

"I wasn't grumbling."

"No? What were you doing then?"

She took another bite from her sandwich and chewed thoughtfully. "I was adding an alternative perspective; balancing your gung-ho, hairy-legged enthusiasm."

"You made it though. The summit of Great Gable and now a seat for lunch with the finest view in England."

"It is a good view. I'll give you that, but this seat is pretty uncomfortable. Don't they do any softer rocks?"

Matt laughed. "No, all the seats come as standard rock-hard. The view though, some people say that the view from down there looking up towards Great Gable is the best, rather than this way round."

"But you don't agree?"

"No. Especially not today, because from up here today you've got a full-length view of Wastwater framed by those screes, the sense of falling away perspective with all the steepness and here, in the foreground, the most beautiful woman in Europe, let alone England."

"What? Oh yuk! You trying to make me puke?"

She pulled a face and laughed at him as she tried to manage her wind-swept hair, tucking a lock behind her ear and straightening her woolly hat while Matt glimpsed her face, glowing after the exposure to the fresh air of the ascent. Her eyes too, he tried not to stare, but they shone like polished jet.

"Hey, young fella! You got some good photos?"

Matt had to drag himself from his reverie. It was Nicky who answered as the question had been addressed to him.

"Yes, I've got loads."

It was the man from the wooden shed which served as a booking office for the lake launches. In his wellies, he scrunched towards them across the loose pebbles. "It's good to see young lads so involved in something. Is it a hobby?"

"Yes, we're going to go back and pin up some pictures and write about them."

The man looked from Nicky to Matt and then back again. "Are you going to take some of these ducks?"

"Yes," said Nicky.

"I'll tell you what then, take a photo of me in all my finery, these are my best wellies after all, take a photo of me and I'll bring you out a bag of food for the ducks. Not bread, but stuff that ducks like. What do you say?"

Nicky looked towards Matt who nodded assent. "Don't forget what you have to say though."

"Thank you," Nicky called after the departing man.

"Good lad."

It didn't take long for all the ducks in the area to realise that easy food was being scattered. They gathered in a squawking, quacking scrummage around Nicky as he flung out some of the seeds before handing the bag to Matt who shouted instructions above the din.

"Don't just point at the whole gang. Fix on one particular duck, try and catch it when it looks up at the camera."

Then he picked up his own camera as providence had landed in his lap.

When all of the food in the bag was exhausted, the ducks soon lost interest and drifted away. Calmness reasserted itself across the lakeshore and Matt stood up to stretch his back.

"Wow! That was all-action. Well done!"

"Where did they all come from? There was hundreds of them. Did you see that scruffy black and white one?

It kept nipping all of the others, biting them and pinching the food."

Matt smiled at the way that the monosyllabic Nicky of the morning had disappeared. "Nipping and biting? The height of bad manners, I'd call that."

"There's someone in our class like that."

Matt was primed to make another joke but then he caught himself.

"What do you mean?"

"One of the boys in our class. He pushes and bites people to get his own way."

"Well, he won't have many friends."

"He does have some friends. If you're his friend, he doesn't bite you."

Matt let this comment settle, giving himself some time to weigh up his next comment.

"Are you one of his friends?"

Nicky did not look at Matt, but he did shake his head.

Seven

"I can't believe you've never had a ninety-nine before."

"No, but now they're my favourites."

Once again, Matt found himself smiling. Kids, so easy to please, it seemed...sometimes. He looked up at the scene before him, at the town which was performing a dress rehearsal for later in the summer when it would be thronged with tourists. Market day with a series of white, canvas-topped stalls lined up like small boats in a marina and a hustle and a bustle around each one. He pointed to the tall building in the middle of the square,

"See that place there, the place that looks a bit like a church...that's where Becky works." Nicky was negotiating his way around a dripping ice-cream and made little response. "It's the Tourist Information Office. People ask her lots of questions and Becky answers them."

Not for the first time did he wonder why he was building up Becky. Was that for Nicky's or his own sake? Becky, who was doing a job well below her capabilities.

"What kind of questions?"

"Well, they are visitors, they ask all sorts of questions about this area. Where are the best places to go and how to get there. Where can they get on a boat to sail on the lake?"

"And Becky knows all the answers?"

"She certainly does."

Matt pulled a huge cotton handkerchief from the pocket of his shorts. "Here, you'd better give your hands and face a rub. You've got ice-cream everywhere."

Nicky took the hanky and wiped. That had not been a telling-off. But Matt was talking again.

"You know that boy you told me about, the one in your class, the one who bites people, he must be spoiling things for everyone, is he? Nobody wants that. Has anyone told your teacher about him?" A dark cloud passed over Nicky, evidently, he was not going to answer. "Well, have you told your mum?"

A further silence. Nicky's earlier exuberance diminished. Matt had entered a no-go area, part of Nicky's world about which he wouldn't speak. Although it had been Nicky who had first brought up the subject. So, when he raised his eyes to make eye-contact, Matt paused, let him speak now if he wanted to.

"You could do that. You could tell my teacher."

Market place busyness continued. Examination of goods took place and transactions were completed. Fruit, veg, fudge, chocolate and sweets were handed over in return for cash. Everyone completed the procedures and stall holders yelled out, "Not many left now." And Matt searched for an answer he could give to Nicky. Something about how complicated life was for adults too, or something about how they all had to follow lines of behaviour. Something that would make sense to Nicky after he had volunteered a snippet about what was concerning him. Reassurance. Where could he muster some reassurance for Nicky?

"I'll tell you what, are those hands of yours clean? Because we'll go back, we'll work on those pictures and we'll have a think about things."

"Are we going to print off some of my pictures?"

"Yes, that's the plan. You can take some home if you want."

"No, I want them on *your* wall."

"Okay, we'll have foxes and ducks mingling together. That should start some quacking. We'll put a fox amongst the ducks."

They stood up from their bench and began their walk with Nicky reaching up for Matt's hand.

It caught Matt's eye as soon as they turned the corner; a five-door, two-litre Jaguar XF with dark red paintwork which stood gleaming incongruously half way along the modest terrace outside his front door.

"Oh Shit!"

"Rude word!" shouted Nicky.

"Sorry, but *shi – it*."

"Mum says rude words."

"Does she? Well sorry again, anyway."

As they approached the car, the two front doors opened on cue and Bill and Wendy, solemn faced, stepped out to join forces on the pavement and then they made a few slow steps towards Matt and Nicky. A doom-laden soundtrack was playing in Matt's head and he had to remind himself that he was on his own patch and these two facing him were the guests.

"So, here you are." It was Wendy who fired the first salvo. "Did you forget that we were coming?"

"Sorry, we got held up. We've been men on a mission." Matt looked down at Nicky as though to include him in the exchange.

"And who is this young man?"

If this was an invitation to speak, Nicky ignored it preferring to hold Bill and Wendy in a steady gaze.

"This young man is Nicky. He lives next door and we've been out taking some photographs."

Wendy stepped towards Nicky, held out her hand and smiled." And I'm Wendy. I'm Becky's mum." She took Nicky's limply proffered hand and shook it, ignoring the sticky remnants of ice-cream on Nicky's palm. "I hope you've got some good photographs you can show me."

"We've got some ducks."

"Ducks! Excellent. I look forward to seeing them. But speaking of Becky, where is she?"

"You'd better come in for a cup of tea," Matt felt that there was a limit to what they could achieve on the pavement. "There's a lot of explaining to do. Come on in, Bill. How you doing anyway?"

"So, that's more or less it." Matt replaced his mug on the table. Becky, he knew, would have used cups and saucers, but Matt thought he had scored an early point by serving the tea in mugs, the Lakeland ones with the Herdwick sheep standing proudly on the front. "I'm sorry if we left you sitting in the car. Were you waiting long?"

"No, not long at all." Bill had hardly spoken. He was weighing up all of the information he had received and assimilating it in his head. "We had a little bit of business to do anyway. When do you think we'll hear from Becky?"

"Who knows? I've tried ringing her but there's nothing doing." Matt dropped his voice, conscious of the fact that Nicky was only a matter of yards away in the small front room watching the tv again. "She's probably turned off her phone in the hospital. I've tried texting."

"I'm sure she'll ring when she can. Don't worry about it," said Wendy, taking Matt by surprise. In all of the explanations he had given and all the patient answering of questions, he'd begun to realise that their conversation lacked its usual edge. Nicky's situation, for instance, being brought up by a single mum who was pregnant again with no sign of the father, would normally have drawn some barbed judgements. Even the unwashed dishes from their late breakfast had escaped censure. All of these murky waters ready to be stirred with a big stick and yet Wendy was at peace. Was it Becky's usual presence in the discussions which added the toxic element? Becky who found herself trying to balance familial pressures with her sometimes-strained loyalty to Matt? In her absence the battle lines had not been so rigidly drawn up. In fact, Bill and Wendy appeared to take speedy cognisance of the minor crisis and had mucked in and coped. Wendy had been a revelation in the way she had responded to Nicky without the condescending tone so often employed by adults in talking to kids.

"So, Nicky, apart from taking great photographs, what else do you do? Football? Are you a footballer?"

"Houses. I build houses." Nicky had soon realised there was no sting in the tail to these questions and he could answer without fear of consequences. "With my Lego. I build houses."

Wendy had decided that she could easily spend some time with this young boy who lived next door to her daughter. Together they had been through the photographs and chosen the six to be printed off and she was happy to take the lead in writing out titles so that Nicky could copy them for the display.

"We're a team, are we not?" she'd said, "A good team."

Now though, Nicky was watching his programme and, in the kitchen, conversation amongst the adults had dried up. Another cup of tea would simply be drinking tea for drinking tea's sake, an attempt to fill endless minutes. They were waiting.

It was Colonel Bogey who finally brought the waiting to an end. Matt's ring tone played as though on a steam organ. As looks were exchanged, Matt scrambled for his phone.

"Becky?"

"Matt? Yeah. Are you with Nicky? I'm with Donna. She wants to talk to Nicky."

"Becky, is everything okay? Are you okay?"

"Matt, will you put Nicky on and then I'll tell you everything."

"Hang on, he's in the front room."

Nicky was favouring a position sprawled across the carpet to watch a smiling young woman grooming a lion.

"Nicky, it's Becky on the phone. She wants to put you on to your mum."

Nicky was reluctant to take his attention away from the screen but he took the phone from Matt.

"Yeah…yeah…okay."

Matt now felt as though he was intruding and he slipped back into the kitchen to be met by expectant looks from Bill and Wendy. He shrugged. "I don't know. Nicky's talking to his mum."

Wendy began collecting the mugs from the table and then put them down again when Nicky wandered in holding the phone. He handed it over to Matt and then spoke to the expectant silence.

"Mum's not bringing a baby home."

Like dropping a broken string of pearls on the floor and not knowing how to react; no-one spoke or moved until Wendy took the few steps towards Nicky to fold him into a hug.

"Oh, you poor boy!"

Matt looked at the phone which had just been returned to him and, even though all of the evidence suggested it would be impossible, tried to maintain contact.

"Becky! Becky!" He looked up at Bill who was closest to him and said, unnecessarily, "The call's ended."

"Ring her back. Try ring back." Redundant in the child hugging episode, Bill could at least show his worth as a man of action.

"She rang here," said Matt.

"Well try call last number."

"Wait on, if they got cut off, Becky will ring back. She won't get through if I'm trying to ring out."

Bill wanting to take charge. Bill wanting to kick-start some action. In the face of Matt's apparent passivity, they were on familiar ground: wilfulness and unspoken opposition.

When Colonel Bogey marched in again with his incongruous ring tone, Matt ignored his split-second triumph and pressed receive.

"Becky?"

"Matt? I've messed up. They're gonna keep Donna in, of course. I jumped into that ambulance without giving a thought about how I would get home. If I get down to the bus station, I can catch the four-thirty to Keswick. It's the last bus. If I miss that I'll have to make my way to Cockermouth for a connection."

"Becky, slow down. You're gabbling. How are you? How's Donna?"

Matt looked at his phone again thinking he'd been cut off for a second time, until Becky's voice picked up again.

"It's been awful. They're looking after Donna but it's been bloody awful. I can't tell you it all now. But we need to talk, we really need to talk. Not now though, I have to get to the bus station in twenty minutes."

"Becky? This is Dad." The phone had been unceremoniously removed from Matt. "I think I caught some of that. Where are you?... The Cumberland Infirmary. Right, stay there. It can't be more than thirty-five, forty miles. Stay there, get to the front entrance or whatever. I'll come and get you."

There. Decision made. Job done. Bill handed the phone back to Matt.

Eight

Becky balanced and then readied herself for the next leap to an adjoining rock, smiling in triumph as she completed her manoeuvre and the spring water gushed below her.

"And for my next trick!"

"Just you be careful on those rocks. Mind the wet ones."

One more jump and she sat down on the grassy bank next to Matt linking her arm into his and snuggling up against his shoulder.

"If I'd fallen in, would you have jumped to my rescue?"

"Like a shot. Any chance to play the hero."

He loved her when she was like this, less intense, playfully dancing between the rocks and the sparkling water and now pressed up against him. She hadn't tied back her hair and it was much too warm for a hat. She looked wild and free, a spirit untamed. Without looking directly at her, he knew she would be smiling.

"I've seen that before."

"Of course you have. It's Ashness Bridge. Mainstay of a million calendars, postcards and biscuit tins."

"It's beautiful."

"Agreed. When God made that he wasn't having a day off, was he?"

They sat and looked at the packhorse bridge which allowed cars to cross from one side of the stream to the other, straining up the steep hill in low gear, crossing the bridge and then pressing on as the single-track road passed around a bend, headed into a wooded area and then slipped out of sight further up the valley.

"That's Derwentwater all the way down there, yes?"

"Yes."

"And there's that big mountain over there, what's that?"

"That big mountain, is a fell and it's called Skiddaw."

"A fell, sorry, I forgot. Are you going to take a photograph?"

"Not today, no. I prefer to come here in autumn or winter. Winter when there's some snow around."

"Some snow, some wintry conditions to stir the soul?"

"Absolutely."

She snuggled closer into him nudging him on his rocky perch.

"Hey! What're you doing?"

"Wrestling you. Trying to topple you."

"What for?"

"To show that I love you."

"Shit! I wouldn't like to see you angry with me."

"To say that I love you and thanks."

"Thanks for what?"

"Thanks for bringing me up here, to the fells, becks and all this *watter*."

They watched another car toil up the hill, negotiate the sharp corner to cross the bridge and then continue with its journey the sound of the engine slowly fading. A crow uttered four hoarse croaks, and scattered across the surrounding fellsides, isolated sheep rooting amongst the bracken issued reminders of their presence with low guttural bleating.

"You sure? You don't want to go back to Manchester?"

"What's in Manchester?"

"It's what you're always telling me. Manchester, the radical city of the north, scene of the Peterloo Massacre, written about by that poetry guy."

"Shelley."

"That's him. A modern city you reckon with good jobs, good jobs for English graduates: copy-writing, arts administration, web content management. What are you doing up here amongst all these sheep?"

"I have my reasons, you daft bugger." She laughed and began another bout of wrestling but he evaded her attempted hold.

"Well, in that case, I've got some news for you."

"News?"

"Yes. House news. We've got the house. Our two-up, two-down, terraced palace is ours. We can pick up the keys and move in from the beginning of the month."

Nine

"Jaguar XF. Two litre, fuel injection engine, five gear automatic. I could give you more details but you don't strike me as a guy for technical info."

Decisions had been made and Matt could do little but concede. Bill would drive through to Carlisle to pick up Becky and Matt would accompany him, sitting and listening to all of the specifications of the car which admittedly, had purred through the streets and then issued some impressive thrust as Bill opened up outside the town boundaries.

"It's a nice car."

Always when Bill and Wendy turned up, he felt diminished. He'd thought of borrowing his mate's van to go and pick up Becky but that plan couldn't hold out against the gleaming red beauty outside their house ready to do service. Let Bill show off his pride and joy. Wendy had declined the trip to Carlisle. Nicky had been collected by Jackie, Donna's mate, and Wendy had said she would stay in the house as she had plans. "Have you seen the state of this place?" and Matt had bristled.

"Relax, Matt," she said, "You've done a great job today. Go and pick up Becky and I'll have a tidy up in here and I'll have some supper ready for you all when you get back."

So, now he sat back in the seductive comfort of the passenger seat as Bill eased the Jaguar past the early season caravans and heavier freight on the A road to Penrith.

"How is the photography business, Matt?"

"Oh, you know, the commissions come in and freelance sales keep a steady turnover. I took some shots this morning; a family of foxes, that should bring in a healthy cheque, I'm hoping."

He was aiming for an easy insouciance. It was the pressure he constantly felt in Bill's presence.

"Sounds a bit piecemeal. A bit uncertain?"

"It can be. Peaks and troughs."

"Have you ever thought about establishing a more stable base?"

"How do you mean?"

A slight pressure from his right foot and Bill accelerated past a dormobile and two sedate saloons on a stretch of dual carriageway before returning to his question.

"Matt, I've been on your website, I've looked at your gallery and yes, I did look at those foxes. I'm no expert, but I think you're a good photographer."

"Thank-you."

"That's an impressive website. You're a good photographer but a poor salesman, marketeer, publicist. Your self-promotion skills need a damned good polish."

"Becky put that website together."

"I thought as much. Is she still writing...?" No answer, so Bill continued, "Yes, it is a good site. How many sales do you make through it?"

Still no answer from Matt. Stressing the positive was one thing, lying was another. He waited for Bill to continue.

"A virtual presence is fine, but up here with all these tourists on tap, have you ever thought about getting yourself some physical footfall? Some gallery space?"

They approached the motorway junction and Bill slowed the car at the traffic lights and picked up speed again as they changed to green.

"Thought about it, yes. Made any progress on that front, no. All of the galleries up here have got sufficient material, thank-you. Any rental space which does become available comes with a massive rental price or prohibitive percentage conditions."

"Catch 22, eh?"

"I think so."

"What if it did somehow become possible?"

"When pigs fly you mean? You know, I'd still think about it very carefully. There'd be a lot of pressure to show glorious Lakeland scenes. What the world doesn't need right now is someone else photographing sunsets over Derwentwater."

"You're a principled man, Matt. I can see why you and Becky got together. Do your principles ever get in the way of things though?"

"Principles? They can be a nuisance sometimes. Do they ever get in the way of *your* business?" Matt wasn't absolutely sure what Bill's business was: property development and management? Whatever, he thought that some of the pressure of this conversation should be transferred to him. "I mean you're so much more the business man than I am, you must come across a lot more situations where you could bend the rules or cut a few corners. Are you speaking from experience now?"

"Ouch! Touchy as well and ready to bite back. Yes, you and Becky are a good match."

"Sorry, I may have overstepped the mark."

"No, don't apologise. I was pushing you a bit and I got what I deserved. I'll tell you what though, business is just like any other walk of life. Sometimes the principles that you've cherished lie shattered at your feet. And do you know what?"

"No, what?"

"At times like that, it's pretty handy if you can make some new principles very quickly. Was it Groucho Marx or Woody Allen who said that these are my principles and if you don't like them, I've got plenty more where they came from."

Matt couldn't ever remember a time when he'd laughed alongside Becky's dad. But nor could he remember a time when they had ever spent any time, one to one, in a serious conversation.

"What does Becky say about all of this? Is she happy? You didn't answer the question about her writing."

Sensible conversation or not, this one had suddenly lurched towards the deeply personal and Bill had lobbed in a question with huge ramifications. What did Bill know? Did he know anything at all? Matt reached for a platitude.

"She's fine."

The comment fell like rubble down a chute.

"Fine, eh? Look Matt, call me an interfering, over-protective father if you like, but I'm picking up signs that Becky isn't fine. This isn't me taking sides, except the only side I'm ever on is for the pair of you: Becky and Matt together, and I think you need to do some talking."

Afterwards, Matt would realise that he had been disarmed and his defences were down. He'd laughed with Bill and he'd listened to him, why else would he have come out with his next comment.

"When I got home this morning, I found she'd been packing her suitcases."

Bill didn't look shocked, or in any way surprised, but he did take his eyes briefly off the road to look at Matt and then paused as he was taking stock.

"Well, that settles it then, when we get to this hospital, I'll drop you at the main entrance and I'll go and find somewhere to park. You know what hospitals are like, I could be ages. But you find Becky and ask her."

"Ask her about …photography?"

It sounded idiotic as soon as he'd said it.

"No, take some time and ask her how she is. She's had a rough day, I'm guessing. Talk to her. Find out what's bugging her. You'll have the time."

Saturday afternoon traffic on the motorway was light and they continued to make good progress for the last few miles albeit in silence now. They passed signs for a service station and then for a junction for Carlisle South. Farmland with a meandering river, newly-built housing and the city emerging before them. Time now for SatNav to take charge.

He found her almost straightaway inside the main entrance to the hospital. It was busy with visitors, hospital workers and high-vis jacketed volunteers going about their business. Others wearing dressing gowns showed little regard for how they were dressed, they would not be going anywhere any time soon. Here to Help, the sign above the volunteers' stall was trying hard, but it had been a long day and smiles were jaded.

Becky though, was there: beautiful, vulnerable, feisty and wrecked, but she was there. Without any kind of preliminaries, he hugged her. He wanted to grab her and not let go but she was unresponsive and the embrace was stiff.

"Dad? Where's Dad?"

"He's looking for parking. It's a bit of a nightmare, he says he'll ring when he's sorted and I said we'd go and find a cup of tea."

"I don't want any tea. I'm sick of fucking tea."

Wounded, he led her away from the bustle. He'd seen a few benches outside and a peaceful garden area to which he started guiding her; that would do.

"Can you talk? Talk to me about anything, Becky. How bad was it?"

Her voice was quiet and he had to lean in to hear her. "It was absolutely awful. Blood everywhere and there was nothing I could do. Why was I even in that ambulance? I was holding her hand and she was squeezing mine for dear life. What do you say to someone who's screaming and shouting all sorts. Everything I said must have sounded really stupid. She's bleeding all over the place and I'm saying that she was going to be fine. I'm sure the paramedics did their best, God, I couldn't do that job, but she had no dignity at all; she was shouting and screaming and all I could say was, 'You'll be okay.' What a complete and utter fool."

Matt reached for her hand. What he wanted now more than anything was some kind of response. This remote Becky, filled with bitterness, was so alien to him.

"Becky, you're being harsh on yourself. You were there for her. You responded straight away. Everyone

120

else just stood on their doorstep wringing their hands. You were great."

"As soon as they got her here," She continued as though she hadn't heard a word that he'd said. "They whisked her away. I tailed after her but I had to sit outside for forever until eventually someone came out and spoke to me asking if I was her partner or sister. Who the hell was I in other words. I told them I was Donna's birth partner, standing in, in an emergency. And it was certainly that. She'd haemorrhaged badly, so badly they called it a near miss. Jeez, she nearly died. But they did let me in to see her eventually, and there she was, sedated I think, with tubes and wires all over the place and she gave me the weakest smile ever, but it was a smile."

"Becky, you did brilliantly."

"She didn't say much to me, but she knew I was there. And the baby, after all that blood and panic, the baby is the sweetest thing I've ever seen."

"You saw the baby?"

"Yes, they had a cot for her next to Donna's bed. It's a girl, a lovely little girl. And Matt, Donna says she's going to call her Rebecca… What's the matter?"

"Becky, Nicky said that the baby wouldn't be coming home."

"What?"

"We thought…"

Ten

At nine hundred and thirty-one metres high it was Skiddaw which towered over their route from the town and dominated every upward glance. A huge presence demanding attention and respect, but Becky who had chosen the route and the destination had another plan in mind. They were heading for Latrigg which was a mere three hundred and sixty-eight metres high. She had her reasons, the day's destination had to be memorable and easily accessible as she had no idea what their walk and planned talk held in store, but she was aware of the worst possible outcome and either way the event would register and resonate. She knew to leave the disused railway line at Briar Rigg and start the ascent up Spoonygreen Lane trying not to look up at the formidable presence of Skiddaw and its cloud-covered summit. On the track of the Cumbrian Way, you should continue climbing through woodland before emerging onto the open land which borders Mallen Dodd keeping an eye open for a footpath which cuts back acutely to the right. It is still a well-defined path but the contour lines are packed more closely together and the walking will become tougher. Time to shorten your stride but maintain a consistent rhythm. Her map reading and fellwalking skills had been well taught.

"Latrigg? Why Latrigg?"

"Because it's one of *my* favourite spots, that's why."

She would say no more. This walk was taking place at her insistence. She had avoided any small talk because what she had to say later was going to be important and she wanted to keep a clear head, to avoid distractions and concentrate. When the footpath took another sharp turn to the left, she knew they had almost reached their goal. And there it was, the prominently sited bench with a view right down over the town, the lake beyond that and up towards the inviting terrors of Borrowdale.

"Is this your favourite view because it comes complete with a bench."

"Yes, why not? We came for a talk, didn't we? So, we should be as comfortable as possible. I don't want to settle my arse on a heap of rocks."

"Every man and his dog comes here. You get walkers in sandals and reluctant kids being dragged by their parents who'll be lost as soon as the cloud drops. Look at the view, all that housing, all those roads and listen to the traffic noise. Mankind and civilisation, all too present. We're not even an hour from home."

"Exactly. If need be, we can pack up and clear off."

She would not riff alongside him, not contribute to his contrary stand. He would not break her mood and that tone of voice made him look at her more closely. He dropped his faux grumbling when his darkest fears were realised.

"Becky, we're not breaking up, are we?

That was when the first tears began to pool in her eyes.

"I think we might be."

"Becky, Becky. No! Why? What do you mean?"

1 2 3

She pulled out a packet of paper tissues from her pocket, tore into the packaging and then extracted one and began to dab at her eyes.

"I told myself I wouldn't cry and I'm hating myself for this now." Then she straightened up. "But I'm okay now. We're going to be adult about this and we're going to talk." She pulled a thermos flask from her mini-rucksack and began pouring coffee into two re-useable cups. "We'll have this coffee and when we're done, we're done."

"You've got this all planned out."

"I have. We can be mature about this."

A cold wind rose up riffling the closely cropped grass. The weak sun which had fought its way through the early morning cloud now disappeared again.

"Zip up your coat Becky. Don't get cold." Yes, it was a bit chilly all of a sudden. She zipped up her coat and pulled the collar around herself. "And start talking, if that's what we're going to do."

"Okay," She took a deep breath, "I've reached a stage where this is not enough."

"You know I'm going to argue with everything you say, don't you? Everything you say, I'm going to dismiss. What isn't enough?"

"And there's the problem right there. Don't argue with me. Let me speak and you listen, because we never do that. We never talk and you never listen. You're always off somewhere else, mentally or physically, you go missing."

"Well, yeah, talking, words, you deal with all that sort of stuff."

"Matt, you can't keep abdicating responsibility. There are some things you have to face up to."

"Such as what?"

"Such as what? I'll tell you such as what." She gave herself a beat to recapture her composure. "Yesterday, I was with Donna and it was the most bloody, beautiful, ugly, inspiring thing I've ever seen. At the end of it all, I was in awe and it confirmed for me, finally, certainly, that I want to have kids. I've always known that…and I've always thought that…I don't know, I've always thought that I wanted you to be the father of those kids."

"Shit!"

"What does that mean? What kind of response is that?"

"I don't know what else to say, Becky. I've told you already, yes, yes, let's have kids. Do you want me to stand up and yell across these fells, *Let's have kids!*"

"I know you said that. I heard you say yes, but what have you done since then? Some months we barely bring in enough to feed ourselves, the house isn't big enough to open up the dining table let alone have kids running about the place. What mental adjustments have you made, Matt? It's fatherhood! What practical steps have you taken to get this to happen? Have you even thought about what it takes to be a dad?"

His coffee had gone cold. He still had half a cup to drink but he didn't dare finish it off or throw the remains across the ground. They were staying until their coffee was finished, he'd been told that. He didn't want to initiate a final parting. He shuffled around on the bench to look at her more closely. He wanted to tell her again how beautiful she was and how much he loved her. Had he not told her these things and was that not enough? He had one hand free, perhaps he could reach across and take hold of hers, or would that just result in her snatching her hand away? Would she get up and begin packing her stuff, begin to march back down the way they had come?

"Becky, there was a practical idea, an ideal route was put forward last night."

Eleven

She'd looked all over for some decent glassware without success. Eventually she found four wine glasses which didn't quite match but they would do. She picked up one of the glasses and held it up to the light and allowed herself a most satisfying tut. What are they like, those two?

Wendy had had a good couple of hours. As soon as Nicky had been collected by Donna's dishevelled, and it has to be said, rather scatty friend, Wendy set to work. She nipped into town to try and find the mini-market to see what delights she could pick up there, but stumbled instead over a nicely arranged supermarket with a delightful choice of goods, a choice which was good enough for her to be able to prepare a roast chicken with salad supper, complete with a baked cheesecake and fruit compote dessert and a nice bottle of pinot grigio to wash it down. This wasn't such a one-horse town after all.

On her return, she rolled up her sleeves to give the small kitchen and sitting room what she expected to be the best spring clean they had ever had. Once the chicken had been roasted and the table laid, everything was looking rather cosy, not elegant but bijou at least. Apart from the wine glasses of course which she picked up and polished again.

And then she was done, except that she was drawn back to the kitchen wall and the impromptu display of photographs with their headings. What a funny little boy that Nicky had been, and yet, he was delightful once he overcame his shyness. Some of his suggestions for headings for the photographs had tickled her, "Sailor wiggling his wellies" for instance and "foxes looking for eggy bread." She laughed again and then just as suddenly stopped because she was looking in detail at some of the photographs which had clearly been taken by Matt. A close up of the boy feeding ducks for instance where he was totally oblivious to the presence of the camera which had caught him fully absorbed. And then there was the spontaneous shot of the boy waving his foot in the air in a clear parody of the boatman pictured earlier. Their daughter's partner was clearly a very talented photographer and Bill was absolutely right in the proposal he was due to make that evening. Wendy checked the time again; they shouldn't be too long now. She would be nice tonight, refraining from any comments which might be construed as judgmental in any way. She would try her very best.

Sitting down for the meal had not been the joyous occasion she'd expected. Of course, it had been a traumatic day, particularly for Becky, but once the good news had been released and an explanation had been given of how Nicky had relayed only part of the news: Mum wouldn't be bringing the baby home *for a day or two yet*, she thought they might have cheered up a bit. She thought she might even receive a little more approbation but that always tended to be her lot, and the rest of them remained sombre. Becky had greeted her with a hug which seemed to be more about profound relief than welcome. She and Matt were apparently at odds and even Bill had been a little withdrawn. But he did propose a toast to the new baby who was going to be called Rebecca, which was a nice touch, but Becky had just held up an empty glass at the toast.

"No wine, and you've only picked at your food. Are you okay?"

"Yes, I'm fine thanks, Mum. I'm just a bit off eating and drinking. It's been that kind of day."

Wendy bit her tongue. Beyond the day's events, Becky did not look well. Peaky, perhaps sickening for something, but Wendy knew not to persist at this point. Any fuss now could tip the balance.

So, at that point, Wendy concentrated on trying to catch Bill's eye and indicate that he should get on with it. Finally, by some process of telepathy, he must have got the message.

"Right, you two. There's something I want to run past you. I'm thinking about expanding my property and small business interests."

"What?" Becky was surprised. "I thought you were looking to cut down on work."

"Yes, I am, but it doesn't mean I'm going to be blind to a good opportunity when it presents itself. Hear me out." He had their attention. Wendy had a barely suppressed smile. "It's a place here in Keswick. A house with a shop front, amazing space, reception rooms, four or five bedrooms and a sizeable garden to the rear."

"Whereabouts is that?" Matt at least was showing some interest.

"Fisher Street. It's a bit out of the main tourist footfall but it still has a lot of potential."

"Is that Maynard's old place? It's a studio photography place, isn't it? Baby portraits, kids in school uniforms, solid families and old generals pointing at the camera and saying 'Your Country Needs You'." There was no response until Matt confessed, "I made that last bit up. It is a bit dusty though." Then he began to fit the pieces together. "Hang on, Bill. Why are you interested in that place?"

"Well, here's the point. I'm not really interested on a personal basis. Not my usual thing, is it? But potential is potential. I'm thinking about buying it and installing a tenant manager, someone with a bit of flair and imagination to shake the place up a bit. Someone, or a partnership, perhaps."

"Oh, for goodness sake, Bill, spell it out. He wants to buy the place for you two." Wendy had been unable to contain herself.

Becky too, failed to keep her composure, "No! No! No!" She stood up pushing over her chair in the process. "That's just typical. You always think you can organise people's lives by throwing around your money. Buying people. No matter that it hasn't dawned on you yet that Matt is a damned good photographer. He doesn't do babies or new school photos, and he's not a shopkeeper."

"Becky! Becky!" Matt was trying to apply some balm to the flaring irritation.

"No, no. Don't Becky me. Why don't you stand up for yourself for once? You're a professional photographer with an impressive portfolio, you don't need this kind of...patronage." She'd made her point loud and clear, so she stepped away from her toppled chair and added, "I've had a horrible day and I'm going to bed."

An awkward silence settled, and Matt, torn between the need for some kind of apology and loyalty to Becky, found no comfort at all in being struck suddenly speechless.

"Well," Wendy was less circumspect. "I haven't seen the likes of that since she was a teenager. I thought she would be pleased. She could at least have stayed to listen."

"She's had a rough day." Matt was taking baby steps towards recovery. "I'll give her ten minutes and then I'll go up and see how she is," and suddenly found that he could move from rueful to appreciative. "Listen, Wendy, that was a lovely supper and I'm sorry it ended that way. Go through to the other room and relax. I'll see to all this. Bill, maybe you could give me a hand with the dishes?"

If Bill had been surprised to be recruited in to dishwashing, he soon rumbled Matt's ulterior motive. Matt wanted to talk? Well, he could do likewise.

"I think you've got me pegged as either a cold-hearted materialist or else a conniving philanthropist always looking to his own advantage."

"Really? Well, which of those *are* you?"

"Neither of them. At least I don't think so. What I would like you to think is most importantly, I'm a father. And no matter how ham-fisted and insensitive I sometimes appear I know what a huge responsibility that is. I'm a father to Becky, that's a job I signed up to for life. Fatherhood, eh? There's no end date on that. Now, do you want to pop that serving dish back in the sink because you've missed some grease there."

The teamwork proved to be effective and soon all of the dishes were washed, dried and put away. The kitchen was shipshape again and Bill and Wendy could make their preparations for leaving.

"Two and a half hours will easily see us home," said Bill. "Give our love to Becky. There's no harm done. Nothing that can't be sorted, anyway."

"Two and a half hours, Matt," Wendy chipped in, "Is that too long a journey for you two, do you think?"

"No, not at all, you might have to lend us the Jag though."

Once again, Matt witnessed Bill's driving style with unsettled awe. Bill's assumption that everything was laid out for his convenience, his mounting of the pavement without compunction with front and back wheels as he completed a three-point turn, the imperious nudge on the steering wheel to engage the power steering and then the heightened thrum of the powerful engine as the huge saloon surged down the street which had never been designed for motorised traffic.

Matt stood for the courtesy of a farewell wave, not sure if the occupants of the car were aware of his continued presence on the pavement or not, or whether they in turn were bothering with any kind of physical gesture. They had completed their mission and dropped their benevolent bombshell. Now, they could seek out the motorway and leave Matt and Becky to sort, sift and salvage a response.

Locking the doors behind him and switching off the lights, he realised that it was still quite early. He slipped upstairs to the bedroom and undressed in the darkened room before lifting the duvet and sliding into bed next to Becky who lay with her back to him breathing deeply. "Becky, Becky."

He could repeat his soft entreaties but he knew that they would continue to be ignored.

Twelve

"I've got no interest at all in photographing weddings and babies. I told Bill that last night after you'd gone to bed."

"You talked to him about it?"

"Of course I did. And I told him that I was also very uncomfortable about him dishing his money out like that. I said I may not have much to show yet, but I would like to make my own way."

"I thought you would say that. I said the same thing but I flew off the handle a bit, didn't I?"

"Just a little bit, yes, but I think everyone realised you'd had a very stressful day. Your mum though, wow! I've never heard her be so sympathetic, so unwilling to judge. She said you looked tired, looked like you needed a lot of support from the people who love you."

Matt paused to let his words settle, to let the breeze to continue to blow around them and for the sunbeams to suddenly burst through the louring clouds.

"Becky, that's me. I'm one of those people. I love you and you've got all of my support."

Becky took the flask out of her rucksack again and removed the top to see if there was any coffee remaining. She shared what was left into both of their cups without acknowledging her stipulation about when the first cup was finished. Then, on second thoughts, she poured all of the coffee from her cup into Matt's.

"Sorry, don't fancy it. I shouldn't have had that first cup."

They were both there talking, that had been the plan and she knew that Matt would not be walking away any time soon. It was he who broached the silence between them now.

"This has been building for some time, hasn't it? I mean, it wasn't just Donna being rushed off to hospital yesterday that kicked all this off, was it?"

"No, not just that. There's all sorts of things. I get frustrated with that job. Part-time hours in a bloody Tourist Information Office selling postcards and telling people to make sure they're properly equipped before they go on the fells while my sparkling English degree sits gathering dust."

"You think leaving home would help that? You were packing suitcases yesterday morning, weren't you?

"I was, yes." There was little point in denial. "I wasn't going anywhere permanent. I just thought I would go down to Mum and Dad's for a while. A few nights maybe."

There was something to be said for an outdoor meeting like this. The space, the air, the opportunity to try and locate that bird that was doing the twittering somewhere, and the natural brake it applied to testy responses. Like now, when Matt surprised himself with his own composure.

"A few nights at Bill and Wendy's? I don't see how that would help. Becky, I know she's your mother and everything, but she drives you nuts."

"I know, all of those simple question loaded with criticism." For the first time that morning, Becky raised a half-smile. *"Are we not using fish knives for the salmon?"*

And Matt leapt at the cue, this small reminder that they did have so much in common, *"Are you going to be in Manchester any time soon?"*

Again, that smile of Becky's, the one that could bring her beautiful eyes into play, that could spread such warmth, the one that he loved so much. But her next comment brought out a reaction which surprised them both.

"Mind you, Bill's not a great hero of yours either, is he?"

"Bill's okay. Bill put me straight last night."

"Yeah, sure he did. Was that before or after he was waving his chequebook around?"

"Actually, gently but firmly, he told me that he respected our insistence on making our own way, of being independent, but he found our constant, now what was the word he used, cavilling, that's it, our constant cavilling about how he used his money to be hurtful and hypocritical."

"Come again?"

"That's what he said. It's every parent's privilege to help their kids along in whatever way they can, and if that's a financial matter, then so be it. Denying him that opportunity, he says, is hurtful."

"And hypocritical?"

"He was smiling when he said this mind, but he said he admired our stand, what he called our moral probity, and not wishing to besmirch this, he would prepare an invoice for our share of the petrol bill yesterday and he would see that Wendy did the same for last night's supper."

"Dad said all that?"

"He did. And I was laughing as well as feeling pretty small. It was the most salutary piece of dishwashing I've ever done."

He knew that Becky had enjoyed the story, he hoped that she was perhaps seeing her father in something of a new light, he hoped also that some kind of breakthrough had just been achieved. It was a hope which was fortified when Becky announced that they should have some lunch and began producing wrapped goodies from her rucksack. She brought out one big pack of sandwiches for sharing rather than separate packages and this too, he took to be a good sign. She'd utilised the remains of the previous night's chicken, and he felt he could safely launch into his first sandwich.

"You not having any?"

"Not just yet. I'm back thinking about Dad. He was still a bit out of order trying to organise our lives like that. Buying a whole house and business? And I knew you wouldn't be interested in taking family pictures."

Matt chewed on his chicken sandwich. There was a small bag of cherry tomatoes and sliced cucumber he could dip into too. When all was said and done, he would rather have been somewhere up on Great Gable, somewhere in that great massif of central Lakeland: Bowfell or Crinkle Craggs, but this would do, he was still out on the fells, still out having the best sort of picnic and still out with Becky who was beginning to laugh and smile, and now he had to perform a volte-face.

"Actually, he told me that he was very disappointed in the way the idea had been presented. Disappointed too that we hadn't given it any consideration."

The memory was vivid. As the one who was drying, Bill seemed able to control the tempo of the operation. When he paused, Matt had to slow down the piling up of wet dishes on the draining board.

"Matt, I had you down as a man of vision, someone who could realise possibilities. So, let me ask you this: what if all the financial considerations were put to one side, imagine they're all sorted, right? And you could move into that property and take charge. You've got a rough idea of the place. What would you do with it? What would be the plan?"

This wasn't altogether hypothetical thinking as Matt had worked through a number of similar scenarios already. He picked out a big glass salad bowl which needed to be dried, as much to give him a few more seconds, some thinking time. He didn't want it to look as though he had all of these plans already, he didn't want it to look as though he was producing pat answers.

"Firstly, I'd totally revamp that window space. I'd take commissions for family photographs, yes, but not stuffy, formal occasions. I'd let kids roll about on the floor and I'd take picture of them wrestling and laughing. I'd make a name for it. *You want something different for you family photos? This is the place to be.*"

"Secondly, I'd use all that space to hold photography workshops. An all-day, or even a five-day photography workshop course in the Lake District. Take home a worthwhile memento of your visit. Limited numbers with individual attention from the tutor, what kind of course fee premium could you put on that?"

"And you'd be the tutor?"

"Yes, of course."

"And while you're being the tutor, who's fronting the business?"

"We'd need it to have a really friendly, welcoming appeal. For anyone that turns up in person, that is. We'd also have to have a massive on-line presence for sales, product marketing and bookings. There's a role there for someone with charisma, someone highly literate with web development and business management expertise."

Bill was smiling at this point. "Absolutely! Have you got anyone in mind for this?"

"Yes, you know, I have, probably the same person that you're thinking of."

Bill put down his tea towel and grasped Matt in a hug of surprising intensity putting the salad bowl that he held in considerable peril. He spoke over Matt's shoulder,

"Matt, we're on the verge. On the verge."

That their relationship had taken on this tactile quality was another surprise but there was no escaping the fact that something very significant had happened and he would need to share it all with Becky.

Becky who had been indisposed the previous evening, who had said little to him that morning but who now sat next to him on their Lakeland perch getting increasingly buffeted by the growing wind. She was looking a little sceptical because she had a reason for not moving just yet.

"You said all that? And you've been hugging Dad? That was quite a cathartic dish washing session you had, wasn't it?"

"Becky, we're alright, aren't we? I mean, we're not going to do anything silly, are we? We're not breaking up."

He paused, he wanted her to say *of course not,* but she said nothing, so he had to continue, "Because I think we should do this, we should take your dad's offer and show exactly what we can do. Me and you together. What a team!"

"I don't know, Matt. There's still the money question. A four or five-bedroom house with a shop front going concern business and a garden in Keswick! I dread to think how much that is."

"You're not persuaded by his helping his kids schtick?"

"No, not at all. The thought of *Daddy's little rich girl* makes me shudder."

"Okay, well I'll tell you what else he said last night, he said that his will takes very good care of Wendy, assuming she outlives him, and other than that, you are the sole beneficiary. Like it or not, it's all coming your way, whenever that day is. It's not something you want to think about, is it? But he's not daft, your dad, you know that. As far as possible, he's going to minimise the effect of death duties and what would really suit him, that hard-headed financial dealer that your dad is, what would really suit him is to spend all that money now. Try this on for size; we'd be doing *him* a favour."

"That's more like it, a little more manipulation."

"Is it? Maybe it is, maybe it isn't, but there's one other thing: having thought about this really seriously, I want to do this. I want to do this with you beside me. I want you to say that you really believe in my photography and we can make a success of the whole deal. Can you say that to me now? You were shouting the odds on my behalf last night. Can you say it now? Can you say it and commit to our future?

Because I know for certain, you'd thrive on this challenge. I'd be on photography, but you'd have oversight of the whole deal; performance review, developmental strategy, you'd be Business Manager and you'd smash it. And it would be us, doing our thing. So, what do you say?

She'd listened to everything he'd said but she couldn't say the words he wanted to hear. She couldn't say anything and the more she tried, the more she failed to conceal her tears. Her whole body shook with sobs.

"What's the matter with me?"

"I don't know. What *is* the matter with you? Come here, let me hold you." He adjusted his position the better to comfort her, to reassure her. "Come here, you'll be fine. It's all been a lot, hasn't it?"

"What has?"

"Everything. So much trauma and drama in a couple of days. You need to rest a bit."

"I think you're right. I can't say the words you want me to say. Of course, I believe in your photography, but I've got other considerations, and until I sort those, my answer will have to be a no."

"Other considerations? What the hell else is there to consider…"

"Okay, let's put it this way…"

"Go on."

"This business manager role you're talking about…"

"Yeah."

"…What are the job terms and conditions? Matt, listen to me, I mean, specifically, what are the maternity rights?"

Thirteen

Matt was amazed by the prospect of possibilities. She'd know every inch of this National Park, she'd have all of the major summits under her belt before she even reached her teens, she'd be completely unfazed by wild camping and wild swimming in the high tarns, thoroughly efficient, in time she would pass on all her knowledge and skills to her younger siblings. With any luck, she'd have her mother's eyes, the dark blue, purple to near black, beautiful eyes, and that vivacious laugh. She'd love all of the valleys, but Borrowdale would be her favourite and the Westmorland Cairn on Great Gable would be her all-time top lunch spot although she would share her parents' unaccountable regard for Latrigg.

She would know how the northern light gets in.

"You want my daughter, or son, because I'm not convinced that it's a girl yet, you want them to become a feral child of the fells? And me, what do I do while the pair of you go gallivanting in the wild? *They also serve who sit at home and wait*?"

"We'll upgrade. We'll get a bigger tent."

"You're not taking this seriously, are you?"

"Of course, I am. You'll be there with us because you love these fells. Why else are we up here now? Just think of the advantages our child will have. Brought up in Cumbria, but not only that, brought up by the best female role model ever; the best mummy. Thriving in the outdoors, yes, but also literate, well-read, articulate and passionate; she'll not only know the fells, but she'll know all your poets too, your Samuel Taylor Wordsworth and Bob Keats."

"You do this on purpose, don't you?"

On purpose? Like he was capable of any rational action at this point when fatherhood beckoned him like a quixotic dream. He couldn't account for this rush which he now felt. This huge emotional swing he'd just undergone, from fearing utter dejection to being besieged by complete joy. As sure as the clouds overhead would soon pass, as sure as the whole view before them would soon materialise with transcendental force, he knew now who he was: Matt Armstrong, partner of Becky Robinson, soon to be father of their child and, what he'd always thought of as being *my* space, would soon become *our* space. He needed to tell her again of his conviction,

"She will be a she, and we're gonna call her Wendy."

"Oh, give over, you daft beggar."

It could have been because of the sun's tardiness in emerging from the clouds or the insistent cold wind, but she gave him a playful thump then closed in to hug him and he knew without looking that she was smiling that smile again, and her eyes, her jet-black eyes, were shining.

Acknowledgements

All of the following have read some or all of this book in manuscript form and all have passed on constructive comments for which I am grateful: Jimmy Andrex, Gareth Durasow, Howard Falshaw, Silvia Pio and Mike Rylance. As critical friends their criticism is highly valued and as friends they are cherished.

This book was kick started at an Arvon Foundation Writer's residential week in Totleigh Barton, Devon where the tutors, Tim Pears and Rachel Seiffert were both perceptive and inspirational.

Jacqui Bassett is owed a great deal of thanks for granting permission for her art work *The Lake Beckons*, to be featured on the cover.

Your Wee Bit Hill and Glen leans heavily on my brother Eddie's Special Study on Carlisle and the 1745 Jacobite Rebellion completed as part of his degree course. A shorter version of this story was first published by Underdog Press with the title *The Calling of the Whaups*.

Calmness, Courage and Duty was first published by Etched Onyx Publications (Nashville) 2024.

Touching the Honey Slow River was highly commended in the Hammond House International Short Story Competition 2023.

The Whole of the Moon was shortlisted in the Historical Writer's Association Short Story Competition 2022.

As always, Julie has steered a steady course through waters both choppy and calm, keeping the full sails strung and the ship afloat. Love to her as always.

About the Author

John Irving Clarke was born and brought up in Carlisle. With a degree from Leeds University and a P.G.C.E. qualification from St Martin's College, Lancaster he began a career in teaching English which took him to schools in Hertfordshire and Nottinghamshire before three schools in Yorkshire. He followed that with a spell of tutoring adult education creative writing classes both online and face to face. Throughout this time, he built up a publication record for poetry, prose and radio drama. His published novels include *Who the Hell is Ricky Bell?* and *Land of Dreams.*

He lives with his wife in Wakefield where they plot visits to see their son who lives and works in New York.

Further details can be found at: www.currockpress.com